Alexander Fergusson

The Laird of Lag

A Life-Sketch

Alexander Fergusson

The Laird of Lag
A Life-Sketch

ISBN/EAN: 9783337012106

Printed in Europe, USA, Canada, Australia, Japan

Cover: Foto ©Andreas Hilbeck / pixelio.de

More available books at **www.hansebooks.com**

THE
LAIRD OF LAG

A LIFE-SKETCH

By ALEXANDER FERGUSSON, Lieut.-Colonel

Author of 'Henry Erskine and his Kinsfolk,'
'Mrs. Calderwood's Letters,' etc.

EDINBURGH

PRINTED FOR DAVID DOUGLAS

MDCCCLXXXVI

PRINTED BY T. AND A. CONSTABLE, PRINTERS TO HER MAJESTY,
AT THE EDINBURGH UNIVERSITY PRESS

————It was the fashion of old, when an ox was led out for sacrifice to Jupiter, to chalk the dark spots, and give the offering a false show of unblemished whiteness.

Let us fling away the chalk and boldly say,—The victim is spotted.

ROMOLA.

CONTENTS

ILLUSTRATIONS

TO THE READER

WHEN there has been recalled to mind that remarkable group of Scottish gentlemen who devoted their energies to forcing upon their unwilling countrymen the views of the last two Kings of the Stuart line; and when it has been said that Sir Robert Grierson was one of them, it hardly seems as though this narrative of the Laird of Lag's career stood in need of further words of preface.

But, in respect of the period in which he lived, it may be affirmed that no subject has gained more by recent research than that of the events of the Covenanting age in Scotland.

Happily, it is now no longer necessary in discussing such topics to employ strong language. The floods of strong adjectives at one time deemed indispensable—on no one side more than the other—whenever the 'Persecutions' were mentioned, happily are seldom met with now. It used to be a matter of conscience and belief. Under such circumstances impartiality was impossible.

A very refreshing change has taken place in this regard during the last few years. The events in Scotland in the latter half of the Seventeenth century can now be spoken of with the fairness that becomes the study of history.

The publication of such works as the *Lauderdale Papers*, recently issued by the Camden Society; and careful and judicious editing like that which Mr. Osmund Airy has bestowed on these books (that deal with the period immediately preceding the one referred to in the following Sketch) have done much to supply material for an impartial opinion.

Plain and candid words giving a large-minded Presbyterian view, were spoken on this subject in the course of the *St. Giles's Lectures*, on the History of the Church of Scotland, in 1880-81. And it is instructive to

hear one of the most learned of
the Bishops of the Episcopal Church
in Scotland, publicly stating the
opinion—which the study of such
works as the deeply interesting
volumes already mentioned, likewise,
brings us to—namely, 'that it was
not so much Episcopacy pure and
simple which was repudiated at the
Revolution as Despotism, which had
taken Episcopacy by the hand, in
order to serve the purpose, not of
true religion, but of a selfish and
unscrupulous State-craft.'

The accounts of the Covenanting
age as we find them, with little
comment, in the contemporary writings referred to, where 'the secret
springs of history may be observed,'

fully bear out the Scottish Bishop's
theory, that however much the Covenanters may be condemned, no fair-
minded and intelligent Episcopalian
can read the history of the period of
restored Episcopacy under Charles
II. and James VII. without a sense of
shame and humiliation.

'It isn't for men to make channels
for God's Spirit as they make channels
for the watercourses ; and say—Flow
here, but flow not there,' quoth
Dinah Morris—and it is true. But
at the period in question, the current
of common justice was held back :
civil liberty was lost.

It is but poor satisfaction to
reflect, as has been pointed out by
a sagacious critic, that what the

Scots suffered at this time from extortion, hypocrisy, and self-ag-grandisement, was entirely at the hands of Scotsmen; some of them men by comparison with whom—it is believed—the hero of this narrative loses little.

Besides the immediate purpose of this Sketch, it is thought that the incidents related will serve to show that in the later years of the struggle, at all events, the idea uppermost and unquestioned was, that a surrep-titious attempt was being made to bring the nation under ecclesiastical subjection to a power more deadly than simple Episcopacy.

And it may not be out of place to note here that—however unscientific the definition may be—it is certain that, in practice, a marked difference was understood to exist between pure Episcopacy and Prelacy; and that such distinction lies at the bottom of the cause of quarrel.

We read, for example (Lightfoot's Works, quoted by Hill Burton, *Hist.* vol. vi. p. 386), that it was only after ' much ado,' and ' great retarding,' that the worthies assembled in conference at Westminster, were able to define what they intended to convey by the ' Prelacy ' they associated with superstition and profaneness. The word as it stood alone was considered ' too doubtful.' Though their deliberations began betimes in the morning, it was mid-

day before they were agreed how
the expression of what they meant
should run.

Ultimately they fell on the definition of the term contained in the
parenthesis that may be seen in the
Solemn League and Covenant (still
to be found among the standards
of the Scottish Church)—' Prelacy;
that is, Church Government by Arch-
bishops, Bishops, their Chancellors
and Commissaries, Deans, Deans and
Chapters, and Archdeacons, and all
other ecclesiastical officers depend-
ing on that hierarchy.'

It was not primitive Episcopacy
they had in their eye. Nor was
it so when, afterwards, ' Black
Prelacy ' was spoken of.

In the preparation of this Sketch, I have been much assisted by Sir Alexander Grierson of Lag; Mr. Thomas Dickson, of the Historical Department of the Register House; Mr. R. R. Stodart, Lyon Depute; Mr. W. F. Hunter Arundell of Barjarg; and Mr. John Carlyle Aitken of Dumfries; to these gentlemen hearty thanks are due.

A. F.

Lennox Street, Edinburgh,
October 1885.

A BORDER MYSTERY.

A

Shallow.—I remember at Mile End Green (when I lay at Clement's inn,—I was then Sir Dagonet in Arthur's show), there was a little quiver fellow, and 'a would manage you his piece thus: and 'a would about, and about, and come you in, and come you in: . . . and away again would 'a go, and again would 'a come:—I shall never see such a fellow.

KING HENRY IV., Part ii.

CHAPTER I.

SOME few years ago an uneasy thought began to impress itself on the minds of the leading men of one of the great branches of the Church of Scotland, that many of the lessons Covenanting times had taught, and stamped—as had been believed—with fire and blood upon men's minds indelibly, were in danger of being wiped away and lost in the rush and hurry of this unrestful age.

Accordingly appropriate gatherings and preachings were ordered to be held on the very spots rendered sacred by the sufferings and death of the Martyrs of the Covenant.

Eloquence could hardly fail to be aroused, and enthusiasm, it was hoped, would be re-kindled by the associations connected with these scenes, and memories revived.

The steps these good people took were not, by
a moment, too soon.   Dean Stanley, in one of the
last of the papers that came from his most graphic
pen, drew a vivid picture in which was shown, in
the midst of a desolate waste of muirland, the
Covenanter's grave, which for ages had been the
object of a solemn feeling of veneration ; but now
the silence and the memories broken by the un-
sympathetic shriek of the excursion train.

Furthermore, it was the experience of the young
Scottish Sterne, in one of his journeys more or less
sentimental, that among the hills of the South-west,
in isolated farms, or in the manse, serious Presbyterian people may be found who recall the days of
the great Persecution, and still hold the graves of
the local martyr in pious regard.   But in towns,
and among the so-called better classes, he fears
that these old doings have become an idle tale.
'Nay,' he says, 'at Muir Kirk of Glenluce I found
the beadle's wife had not so much as heard of
Prophet Peden.'[1]

But the railways are no more to blame for all
this than was the North mail-coach, with its 'four
frampal jades,' according to Mr. Crystal Croft-
angry's opinion, answerable for the 'gadding,' and

[1] *With a Donkey in the Cevennes*, p. 184.

the want of originality and individual character which began to be apparent in his day. It would perhaps be more correct to blame, among other causes of this falling away, that 'passion for individual liberty,' and 'pursuit of personal opinion' that have been indicated as marked characteristics of our time.

And doubtless there are some who will agree with the decent old woman, who, tramping the country all for love, called on the present writer to give notice of one of the meetings above mentioned to be held, literally and figuratively, in view of the Bass Rock, that,—'in thae days there's fully mony modern principles.'

It is the object of this Sketch to gather together certain details concerning a remarkable man of the Covenanting age; some of the legends connected with his career which were afloat in the Border districts of Scotland some forty years ago, but now well-nigh drifted away; and, as far as may be possible, to conserve them. For these traditions have more than an ordinary interest, seeing they relate, in the first instance, to a very memorable period of Scottish history; and secondly, to one of the most striking pictures drawn by Sir Walter Scott, into which he has introduced some of the

most weird and fascinating passages that ever
came from brush or pen.

Throughout the South and West of Scotland
there is no name that has attained such an evil
notoriety as that of Grierson, the Laird of Lag, the
Persecutor of the Covenanters.   There is many a
grim story current in those parts regarding—
amongst others—Irving, the 'wild Laird of Bonshaw;' and of General Dalyell, who introduced to
Scotland that 'new invention,' the thumbikins,
and other novelties, with a barbarity of manner
acquired during his service in the Muscovite
army.   John Graham of Claverhouse and his
dealings with the Presbyterians in the Southern
Counties have been the subject of innumerable
writings, and of the most diversely varying opinions.
A great historian has described, in a well-known
passage, the 'peculiar energy of hatred' in which
his name is held.   But in those districts the name
of Lag has been perhaps better abused than that of
Claverhouse himself.   This is not to be wondered
at, seeing that the scenes of his exploits were for
the most part in Nithsdale and Galloway, his own
country, and in many cases the sufferers were
persons who were looked upon as his own neigh-

bours. 'His gripping claws were made of steel,'
they said—

'Crooked, hard, and sharp,
They pierced men's substance to the heart.'

If it be indeed the test of a neighbour that he
should 'have mercy,' then, in the popular estimation, was Lag emphatically unneighbourly. Strong
feeling is apt—at all events in these districts—to
run into the supernatural; and it was so in his
case. Natural everyday language was tame to
express the depth of feeling that the old persecutors—and Sir Robert Grierson of Lag above
them all—evoked.

Some forty years ago, or more, it was common
in many of the houses in Dumfriesshire and
Galloway to commemorate annually the evil deeds
of the Laird of Lag. They used to represent him
in shape of beast as hideous as the ingenuity of
the performer intrusted with the part could make
it, without wandering far, however, from a conven-
tional model, which it was understood should be
adhered to.

This is how it was done in my mother's house,
and we were singularly fortunate in possessing in
our old nurse, Margaret Edgar, an *artiste* who
had made the part her own, and her name famous

by reason of her wonderful impersonation. She was known throughout the country-side for the manner in which she could 'play Lag,' as the phrase went. Her make-up and her acting were excellent alike. In dressing for the part she used to take a sheet, or blanket, or some such covering, which was drawn over her head and body, only the feet and hands being left out. But the one chief point, on which the individuality of the monster depended, was the head, which was invariably composed in one way, no scope for fancy being permitted. The kitchen implement called in Scotland a 'potato beetle,' which is a large wooden pestle, the handle pretty thick, and between two and three feet long, and ending in a ponderous oval head, was entirely covered by strips of cloth being wrapped round it; eyes were drawn upon it, and pieces of fur sewed on for eyebrows; long ears and a mouth were added, the long handle of the instrument forming an imposing proboscis. This structure was fastened to the head of the performer, who moved on hands and knees; the result was a quadruped resembling a combination of the tapir of Borneo and South American ant-eater, strongly conveying an impression as of a 'character' escaped from a mediæval miracle play. The Abbot of Unreason would have been proud of such an attendant in his train.

The creature was then supposed to follow the evil instincts of its bad original by performing, to the best of its ability, vicious tricks, to the terror of youthful spectators, and the admiration of older critics, if the part were well played.[1]

Margaret Edgar possessed the skill needed to give life-like movements to the beast, and to keep up the character of *ferreting* and *listening* implied by the long nose and ears. She threw into her reading of the part an amount of cat-like inquisitiveness and a determination recalling the restless and unwearying malignity of the original that made the blood run cold of old and young.

[1] At this time there was a wealth of histrionic power among our humble neighbours. *The Gentle Shepherd* used frequently to be given, just as Allan Ramsay penned it, to an appreciative and delighted audience in an old unused barn. The character of '*Mause,* an old woman supposed to be a witch,' was invariably supported by Davie Shearer, our cobbler. He would sometimes travel as far as Annan, or beyond it, on invitation, so widely spread was his reputation in the part. On one occasion he was met as he was on the point of starting on one of these journeys, and was asked where he was going. He replied— 'I'm awa to Ecclefechan to play *Mause;* an' I'll no be back this wee while; there's a man doun there that's awin' me siller, an' I'm just gaen to *eat it aff him.*'

The head and dress being in readiness, a suitable
night had to be chosen for the appearance of the
Laird, usually about the time of Halloween, when
minds are atune with things unearthly. On some
dark November night—for there was some artistic
feeling displayed—when the wind off the Solway
swept in gusts over the dismal and dangerous
Lochar Moss, making the branches of trees to groan,
and the windows of the old house rattle, the Laird
of Lag might be looked for. Then, the company
seated, and the dining-room being left sufficiently
dim and mysterious by the unsnuffed light of a
couple of the miserable 'moulded' candles of those
days, a moaning most melancholy is heard, and anon
the door is slowly opened, and the end of Lag's long
nose appears, then the glaring eyes and long ears
of the creature, who proceeds, with stealthy steps
and head on one side, to listen for sounds of a
house-conventicle, and to smell out Covenanters
under the sideboard and other likely places. The
performance usually ends with an attempt to
pounce on, and capture, a little *Whig body* with
frills round her ankles according to the fashion of
the period. The memories of Drumclog were all
unavailing in presence of this fell Prelatic beast.

Whether in this ancient rite there was any

allegorical meaning, or allusion intended to that dread *Beast* under whose claws it was supposed Scotland had fallen at one time, it is impossible to say. But it is certain that anything more striking, not to say appalling, to young minds can hardly be imagined. If there was with the originators of this custom any idea of inducing the children to ask their parents what they meant by it, nothing could have been devised to answer the purpose better. There was for us in the very name of Lag —besides something quaint in the sound—a terror and a weird fascination, which have not altogether vanished at the present day, when the associations and historical facts connected with it are more fully understood.

GRIER OF LAG.

And first march'd furth the Galloway men,
    Of the antient Pictes they sprang,
Their speares a' sae bright an' bucklers strong
    For many myles yrang.

BATTLE OF CUTON MOOR.

CHAPTER II.

THOUGH the Grierson family cannot claim to have been one of those noble houses whose *rôle* it was to make Scottish history, yet this ancient and knightly race was considered worthy to mate with such and, in a lesser degree, they amply fulfilled their part, for or against their Sovereign, as the exigencies of the times and Border politics demanded. It is not necessary to go through the family records to show how active and willing they were, ever ready to bear their share in most of the stirring deeds on the Borders in the old time—when the long swords rested uneasy in the scabbards, when tempers were as keen as the swords—and not so long.

There appear to be even more than the usual number of vague and unsatisfactory traditions regarding the origin of this family. It is said the ancestors of the Barons of Lag held lands in the shire of Dumfries and in Galloway in Malcolm Caen Mohr's reign; a descent from a brother of King Malcolm II. is also mentioned in the family 'tree.' It is likewise there stated that George de Dunbar, Earl of March, granted the lands of Airde in Dumfriesshire to the Griersons by a charter dated at Dunbar in 1400; while the lands of Lagg are said to have been similarly given by Henry, Earl of Orkney, in 1408. A charter, or confirmation, of the same lands is dated 1473, in the reign of James III., in favour of Roger, son of Vedast Grierson.[1] But, however, these facts may be, it is understood, by those best able to form an opinion, that, though many of the Galloway families are believed to be of Celtic origin, there is no evidence or foundation for the

[1] *Conf. Accounts of the Lord High Treasurer of Scotland*, 1473-1478, where such an arrangement in favour of 'Wedast Gresonne of the Lag' is mentioned. The family tree, a very unsatisfactory production of recent date, likewise shows that a certain 'Sir John M'Rath de Lacht' granted a charter [no date] to his cousin, Grierson of Airde, of the lands of Lagg, etc., 'for monies paid to him in his great necessity.' This charter is said to have been witnessed by 'William, Abbot of Holywood, Sir William de Douglas de Drumlanrig, and Thomas de Kirkpatrick de Kyllosbarne [Closeburn];' and, being so well witnessed, is deserving of mention.

story commonly current that this family was an offshoot of the Highland family of MacGregor, descending from the second son of the 'lame Lord of MacGregor,' the friend and ally of Bruce.[1]

About the middle of the fifteenth century the head of this family had married Isobel de Kirkpatrick, and with her got the lands of Rockhall,[2] not far from Dumfries, from which the family take one of their designations.

At Sauchieburn, where in 1488 the unfortunate King James III. was defeated (and later in the day treacherously murdered), having failed to put down an insurrection of his southern nobility, Roger Grierson was wounded. Whether or not this was in the king's cause does not appear; but as the great majority of the chiefs from Liddesdale and Annandale were in arms to help the Homes and Hepburns, with whom the quarrel began, it is probable that he was among the rebels. Another Roger after him was killed at Flodden; and Cuthbert, one of *his* three sons, was killed in battle.

---

[1] See Douglas's *Baronage*.

[2] In the Inventory of Rockhall writs, the following entry occurs—'Imprimis, a Precept by Isobell Kirkpatrick, Lady Rockhall, for infefting Vedast Grierson, her son, in the lands of Rockhall, dated 4th May 1468.'

About the same period, lived a very remarkable
man, in another line, who is supposed to have
been a member of this family, John Grierson,
a Dominican friar, who was Principal of King's
College, Aberdeen, and head of his order.

In 1567 the Roger of that time took part with
the nobles associated for the support of the authority of the infant king, James VI. The Laird
in 1570 joined Lord Maxwell and a number of the
Nithsdale chiefs and burgesses of Dumfries in
resisting an incursion from the other side of the
Border, under Lord Scrope and Simon Musgrave,
by command of Elizabeth, who had ordered the
country to be ravaged, on account of the supposed
sympathy of the people of those parts with Queen
Mary. After various vicissitudes, the fight ended
in victory for Musgrave who, of course, improved
the opportunity by *lifting* and driving across the
Border, at the spear's point, everything with horn
or hoof that came within his reach; the hope of
such a conclusion had doubtless lent attractions to
the raid in the first instance. The haystacks also
would certainly have been compelled in the same
direction if only they had ' had four feet,' according
to the pithy speech of ' auld Wat of Harden'; for
there was a wonderful unity of sentiment in such

matters on both sides of the Marches. Maxwell and the other Scottish leaders with difficulty found refuge in the intricacies of the Lochar Moss.[1]

The son of the last-mentioned Lag, with many others of the Nithsdale chiefs, as Closeburn and Drumlanrig, were bound to Lord Maxwell by ' letters of manrent,'[2] a form of bond (a specimen of which may be found in the *Border Minstrelsy*), in which they, in consideration of the protection to be afforded them by their powerful patron, engaged during their lives to take his part against all opponents, the Sovereign ' allanerly except.'

Consequently, in 1593, he joined the Maxwells, and took with him, it is said, fifty-four horsemen on the memorable occasion celebrated in Border tale and ballad, when the great Nithsdale Baron,

---

[1] Lord Scrope, in reporting these proceedings, states that his first encampment on the Scottish side was at *Heclefeagham*, from which we may infer that the little village of Ecclefechan was as great a stumbling-block to the Saxon, in the sixteenth century, as it has been found to be in the nineteenth.

[2] In the bond of manrent by ' John Greyrsone of the Lag,' dated 23d March 1549, the laird undertakes to be . . . ' leill and trew man to ane nobill and mychty lord, Robert lord Maxwell;' and he says, ' I sall tak his afald trew and uprycht pairt wyth myself, my kin, fryndes, men and servands and all thai I may styr, on hors and fute.'—*Book of Caerlaverock*, by W. Fraser, LL.D.

with some fifteen hundred followers, and bearing the royal standard, as Warden of the Western Marches, encountered the Johnstones of Annandale, with eight hundred, at Dryffe Sands. Though far superior in numbers, the Warden was signally beaten, entirely through the clever tactics of the Laird of Johnstone, who used on this occasion a device which has proved in more recent times as effective against the cattle-lifting Beloochees on the borders of Upper Sinde as it did against the like-minded *reivers* of Nithsdale. The Lairds of Lag, Closeburn, and Drumlanrig escaped by the fleetness of their horses, but the old and grey-headed Lord Maxwell, 'a tall man and heavy in his armour,' was stricken from his horse and died, under the sword of a victorious Johnstone; or, according to local tradition, from a blow dealt him with the ponderous keys of her tower by Dame Johnstone of Kirkton, who, issuing with her maidens from her stronghold to help her wounded kinsmen, found the old man lying in a helpless state under an old fir-tree.

In revenge for this defeat, and the death of his father, Lord Maxwell's son, fifteen years after, most treacherously murdered the head of the rival family, Sir James Johnstone of Dunskellie, for

which ill deed Maxwell had to fly the country. It
is in reference to this that the fine old poem, so
much admired by Lord Byron and Sir Walter
Scott—'Lord Maxwell's Good-night'—was composed. According to another tradition, before
Dryffe Sands, a reward of a five-pound land had
been offered by the Laird of Johnstone for Lord
Maxwell's head or hand. The reward was, it is said,
claimed by a Johnstone, the old lord having lost
the hand which he held up asking for mercy at the
point of death. The following lines in the poem
refer to this incident, though there is no historical
evidence to justify the accusation they convey—

> 'Adieu! Drumlanrig, false wert aye,
>   And Closeburn in a band!
> The Laird of Lag frae my father that fled
>   When the Johnstone struck off his hand!'

Still, though these Griersons were a rugged and
unruly race, ever ready to give, and take, a fair share
of the proverbial 'Lockerbie licks,' their authority
and that of other Border gentlemen was mainly
what the king had to depend on for the preserva-
tion of order in a district where hereditary instinct,
imagination, and tradition had combined to produce
a restless and turbulent population.

Accordingly, James vi., the shrewd King of Great

Britain, in his wisdom drew up a 'List of such as
are most fitted and have most interest to do his
Ma^tels Service for Commissioners in the Midle
Schyres: To be authorized by themselffes and
ther Deputeis for apprehending of Fellowis and
Fugitives.' Among the number of Border chiefs
intrusted with this duty appears the name of
Sir Robert Grierson of that day.[1]

The wife of the last-named Sir Robert was
Margaret,[2] eldest daughter of Sir James Murray
of Cockpool and Cumlongan. This Sir Robert

---

[1] Both sides of the Border were provided for in this arrangement, and amongst those named are :—

'On the Scottish syd :—William, Lord Marquess Douglas;
Robert, Erle of Nithisdale; John, Erle of Annandale; William,
Erle of Queinsberrie; Lord James Johnstone; Sir Robert
Grierson; Sir John Maxwell of Conheath.'

'On the English syd :—Thomas, Earl of Arundell and Surrey;
Algernon, Earl of Northumberland; Sir John Fenwick; Sir
Ritchard Graham; Sir William Carnaby; Sir John Lowther;
Sir Roger Witherington.'—*The Earl of Stirling's Register of
Royal Letters*, 1630; privately printed, Edin., 1885.

[2] There is some uncertainty at this point of the family history
from the fact that the lands of Cockpool did not come to the
Griersons but to the Murray family (to which Lord Mansfield
belonged). It is supposed that the three sons of Sir Robert
above mentioned may not have been the children of the heiress
of Cockpool, but of another wife of Sir Robert whose name is
not known.

Grierson had three sons, namely Sir John, of Lag;
William, of Barquhar in Kirkcudbright; and James,
of Largangley in the county of Dumfries. Young
Robert Grierson, Sir John's son, a minor, was successively under the tutorship of his two uncles;
but he did not live long to enjoy his paternal
estates. He died at Bath on the 17th March
1666, at the age of eighteen.

He was succeeded by his cousin, Robert Grierson, son of the Laird of Barquhar and his wife, a
daughter of Douglas of Mouswald.

This was the notorious Lag of whom we have
to speak. Sir Robert Grierson, Knight, married
the Lady Henrietta Douglas, sister of William,
first Duke of Queensberry, daughter of James,
second Earl, and his wife, Lady Margaret Stewart
of Traquair.

In the early part of the 17th century it appears
that a change was made in the form of name of
this family, which alteration continued through
one or two generations.

Many of the Highland clans were by royal
authority put under such discipline for their irre-
gularities as threatened extinction.

The clan MacGregor had been specially pro-
scribed for their outrageous conduct. 'Thieves and

lawless limmers' was the 'Parliamentary' language used in regard to them in the old Scottish Acts.[1] Failing sureties, to be placed on the south side of the Forth, 'they were to be pursued with fire and sword, as enemies of God and man.' It was penal to baptize with the name of MacGregor.

Therefore, although there may have been in reality no connection with the Highland tribe, it seems the Griersons, to sever themselves as much as possible from the imputation of such undesirable relationship, resolved to call themselves *Grier ;* the original name being unpleasantly like Mac-Gregor.[2] This step seemed even more expedient

---

[1] By the first Parliament of Charles I. was passed—' A strict Act against the *Clan-Gregour*, ratifying all former Acts against them, suppressing the name, and obliging them after 16 years of age to make compearance yearly, the 24. of July before the Council, to find caution,' etc.—*Index to Scots Acts*, by Sir James Steuart, Her Majesty's Advocate, 1707.

[2] The remarkable speech of Sir George Mackenzie, Lord Advocate, may be remembered in this connection. When Sir James Stewart, Provost of Edinburgh, and his son, the future Lord Advocate of Queen Anne's reign, were 'forfeited' during the troubles in the time of Charles II., Sir George is recorded to have said in open Court,—' This family are not Stewarts, their father was a *pair-legged MacGregor*, and changed his name when he came to town because of the Act of Parliament, and these *forfault* Stewarts are all damned MacGregors.' There were, of course, no grounds for such an assertion.

when, in the course of events, it was deemed necessary to call for the services of the Highland clans
to put down the Covenanters in the South-west.
When these—the Highland Host, as they are called
in history—retired to their hills, their retreat was
necessarily slow, laden as they were with many a
gridiron, pot, and blanket, the plunder of Lowland
homesteads. The Highlander was the locust and
cankerworm of those days, and the Griersons were
still less proud of those they may have believed to
be their cousins from the North. Throughout
the career of our hero, he was, apparently, as often
called ' Grier ' as Grierson.

THE WHITE HORSE AND THE
BLOOD-RED SADDLE.

——Now the Devil is come down in great wrath as knowing his time is but short, and therefore exerting all the energy of
the venom and violent craft and cruelty of the Dragon and
Anti-Christ, *alias* Pope, his Captain General, is now universally
plying all his hellish Energies to batter down and bury under
the Rubbish of Everlasting Darkness what is left to be de-
stroyed of the work of Reformation. . . . In all the Churches
of Europe the Witnesses of Christ are a-killing.

A Hind Let Loose. 1687.

CHAPTER III.

DURING the later years of the Persecution, there were three names which inspired the most unfeigned terror throughout the whole of the South and West of Scotland; these—as has been said—were 'Claverhouse,' 'General Dalyell,' and 'Lag.' Each of these men formed, not inaptly, a type of the different classes of officers at whose hands, while they aimed at the suppression of rebellion, the country suffered so grievously. John Graham of Claverhouse, the illustrious commander, indeed stood alone, and could be classed with no other. His portrait has been drawn from every possible point of view, but these need not now be discussed. Of General Dalyell we have a grotesque but apparently truthful delineation, in the record of him by one of his officers, Colonel Creichton, preserved, oddly enough, among the writings of Dean Swift. He had served long in the Russian army, and had brought home with him the coarse manners which, combined with the queer figure he presented with long beard down to his waist, and big boots impervious to earthly bullets, made him a more striking than a pleasant figure.

In Sir Robert Grierson we have one of the most active of the numerous class of country gentlemen and magistrates who administered sharp justice, and aimed at the punishment of rebellion in their respective districts. He was considered to show an excess of zeal in carrying out these objects, which could only proceed from an intense enjoyment of the work in hand. Macaulay's words regarding Claverhouse, which have been so much cavilled at, describing him as a leader, ' violent of temper, obdurate of heart,' will, it is believed, by the great mass of the people of the South of Scotland, be considered equally to apply to him, as well as several of the other peculiarities popularly attributed to Viscount Dundee. If, as has often been alleged, one of the characteristics of this age be the rehabilitation of objects fallen in public estimation, a notable opportunity for such an effort presents itself in the case of Lag.

It is intended here, however, merely to set down, as impartially as may be, some of the scattered notices regarding him, as the old writers have given them, and with little comment; and to allow the reader to judge for himself, if not how far the name which the hero has earned for himself is deserved, at all events on what the popular opinion is founded.

The first appearance of the Laird of Lag was during the most tyrannous period of Lauderdale's administration. The Highland Host had returned to the North laden with booty gathered to the detriment of the disaffected Presbyterians. Still the ends of the Government seemed no nearer being attained. Fresh garrisons were appointed, new judges were named, as the principal Sheriffs were found wanting in zeal. In Wigtownshire Sir Andrew Agnew named as Sheriff-Deputes the Lairds of Lag and Claverhouse, in the hope of satisfying the requirements of Lauderdale.[1]

The point of time at which Lag and his illustrious colleague appear on the scene, was that juncture at which the edge of the old Covenanter's sword, on which, by certain gaps, the progress of the persecution was recorded, showed *nineteen* of

[1] *History of Galloway,* ii. 212.

these notches, representing in grim fashion the lapse of that number of the twenty-eight years which made up the tale of that memorable period.

1679, the year of Archbishop Sharp's murder, Drumclog, and Bothwell Bridge, was one of the most remarkable in the history of the persecution. In that year it is that the Laird of Lag first comes prominently into notice, as the zealous assistant of Claverhouse, who, having in the previous year returned to Scotland from serving in France and Holland, had been commissioned to put down with the strong hand the rebels, at this time beginning to give fresh trouble in Nithsdale and Galloway.

It was of the utmost consequence, as one may readily conceive, that before Sir Robert proceeded to enforce compliance with the orders of the Government in the districts under his authority, he should have his own house and estates in perfect order. And, in fact, he did take the most effectual means that no one should be able to note any beam in his eye whilst he was intent upon improving the vision, as regards the requirements of the law, in the persons under his jurisdiction as a magistrate.

There has very recently been discovered a very

formal document, a bond drawn up by Lag's desire, and dated the 18th day of February, 1678, by which the tenants and all connected with the estates, with singular docility, engage to conduct themselves in a manner that shall be pleasing to their superior.[1]

Whether in this case Sir Robert took a tender course or round-about way of coming at the conscience of his dependants, or whether it be ' the mere confession of the mouth ' that we have in the following document, it is impossible, with certainty, to say. It is very comprehensive, duly signed, witnessed, and completed with every notarial formality ; albeit apparently only two of the retainers could write. Thus it runs :—

' Wee, William Wright in Rockhall toune, Andrew Scott y^{re} [there], John Burtane y^{re}, Robert

---

[1] It appears that the Duke of Queensberry scarcely had his people in such perfect order. At a later stage of the struggle he writes to his cousin, Douglas of Dornock :—' Andrew tells me of a field Conventicle has been lately held in the head of Sanquhar. . . . I have ordered Andrew to try who was at it, especially my tennants, and send me an Account of all so soon as possible. And it's wonderful that these rascalls, tho' they regard not my prejudice, will need destroy themselves and their poor families. And when nothing of that kind is heard in the Country, that it should be in my interest, and my tennants only Chargeable with it, you ar sure cannot be verrie pleasant to me.' Again he writes :—' Mynd the list of disorderlie people in my Bounds.'

Robson, yʳᵉ, Richard Lewars yʳᵉ, John Irving yʳᵉ, Thomas Wright in Mylneholme, Mathew Dickson in Woodsyde, Bessie Letimer yʳᵉ, Nicol Snadown yʳᵉ, Mathew Dickson in boghall, William Scott in Gattonhirst, James Rule smith in Rockhall, John Brainyian in Woodsyd, John McGiltroch in Collyn, Jannet Currie (and several others),

'Faithfullie binds and obliges us, our wyffes, barnes, servants, and cotters Sall be noe wayes present att any conventickles or dysorderlie meetings In tyme cumming but sall walk orderlie and in obedience to the law under the paynes and penalties containd in the actis of Parlat maide there against, and ffurther yhat wee sall not Resett, Supplie, commune wᵗ forfault persones, intercommñed ministeres, vagrant preatcheres, but sall doe our outmost Indevor to apprehend these personnes : Consenting thir presentis be . . . Registrat in the books off privie counsell. . . .

' Att Rockhall place yhe eightene day off ffeberwarie Jaj vi c Seventie eight yeares, etc.'

It is probable that Lag's first communication with Graham was connected with the exploit described in one of the letters of Claverhouse. He had, on arrival in Dumfries, been much annoyed to find that the far end of the bridge over the Nith was in Galloway, whither he conceived his commission did not extend, and that, consequently, conventicles could be held with impunity 'at his nose,' as he expresses it. This was soon remedied. At the other side of the water Sir Robert Grierson held authority as a principal landholder of Troqueer parish. With such sympathy, and the powers of the Acts of Council, the matter of a meeting-house was easily disposed of. Claverhouse describes the building as a good large house 'about sixty foot of length; they had put up stakes alongst every side, and a *hek* and *manger* to make it pass for a byre,' but the Steward-Depute did his duty well, and —'so perished the charity of many ladies.'[1]

Sir Robert Grierson must at this period have been, as appears from the Dumfries Council Minutes, in constant communication with Claverhouse; and in his letters, and in the records of the time, the Laird of Lag is mentioned repeatedly as an active magistrate; at one time making arrangements for the quartering of the troops, at another sitting with other magistrates for the disposal of prisoners as they were brought in.

Early in 1681, under the Duke of York's rule,

[1] *Memorials of Viscount Dundee*, by Mark Napier, ii. 190.

military courts were established for the administration of summary justice in Galloway. While Cornet Graham, brother of Claverhouse, held one at Dalry, another of a similar nature was established at Kirkcudbright by Grierson of Lag. According to Wodrow, much injustice was suffered through the unfairness of these judges.

The famous Test Act was passed by the Scots Parliament at one sitting, on the 30th August 1681. While it purported to be a defence against Popery, this Act, the enforcement of which on the people became a chief duty of all officers intrusted with the carrying out of the law, gave satisfaction to few. Its ambiguous terms were understood only to mean passive obedience to anything the semi-Popish Government might direct. It has been well and concisely described, in its working, in the following passage:—' It was seen by all parties to be a mass of inconsistencies, which neither Papist, Episcopalian, nor Presbyterian could honestly sign. This made it, however, in the hands of the Duke of York and his advisers, only a more pliable instrument of tyranny, a shelter for the lax, and a terror to the upright conscience.'[1] Popularly it

[1] *Memoir of Lord Stair*, by Æ. J. G. Mackay, LL.D., Edinburgh, 1873, p. 149.

was understood to herald the return of Popery
with all the attendant evils; some of which are
quaintly described in a neat passage[1] in the poems
of Mr. William Cleland, Lieut.-Colonel to my
Lord Angus's Regiment.

The Earl of Argyle, refusing to take the oath,
was tried, condemned to death for treason, and
narrowly escaped with his life. Some eighty of
the Episcopalian clergy, on account of it, lost their
benefices, and had to seek shelter in England.
The Earl of Nithsdale refused to take the Test,

[1] ' For I am vertie apt to think
    There 's als much Vertue, Sonse, and Pith
    In *Annan* or the water *Nith*,
    Which quietly slips by *Drumfries*,
    Als any Water in all *Greece*.
    For there, and several other places,
    About mill-dams and green brae-faces,
    Both Elrich, Elfs, and Brownies stayed,
    And green-gown'd Farries daunc'd and play'd.
    When old *John Knox* and other some
    Began to plott the Baggs of *Rome*
    They suddenly took to their heels
    And did no more frequent these fields;
    But if *Rome's* pipes perhaps they hear
    Sure for their interest they 'll compear.'

—*Effigies Clericorum; or a Mock Poem on the Clergie when they
met to consult about taking the Test, in the year* 1681. Printed
A.D. MDCXCVII.

and was deprived of his office of Steward of Kirkcudbright. Sir Andrew Agnew of Lochnaw declined the Test, and was succeeded as heritable
Sheriff of Wigtown by Claverhouse, his brother,
David Graham,[1] being appointed conjoint Sheriff;[2]
while Viscount Kenmure, for the same reason, was
also replaced in his hereditary office by Graham of
Claverhouse. With the authority thus acquired,
Sir Robert Grierson and others were employed in
enforcing the obnoxious Act. Thus, during 1683,
Lag held a court at the Old Clachan of Dalry,
principally for this object. An Act of Council
passed a little later provided that the 'thumbikins,'
then recently introduced, were to be used.

By another Act of Council, passed in August
1683, which directed that all sentences of death
were to be executed within three hours after being
passed, owning the Covenant, and unsatisfactory
answers regarding opinion on the matters of Bothwell Bridge and Archbishop's Sharp's death, were
constituted capital offences.

---

[1] David Graham ultimately became third Viscount of Dundee,
the second viscount having died in infancy within three months
of his father's death at Killiecrankie.

[2] *Hist. of Hereditary Sheriffs of Galloway*, by Sir A. Agnew,
Bart., 1864, p. 396.

These were the instructions the Laird of Lag
had to carry out in the court he opened in the
parish church of Carsphairn, assisted by Mr.
Peirson, the curate, a man who had rendered himself most obnoxious by his informations against the
Covenanters—the same who was afterwards shot
in a brawl connected with his too active enforcement of the Abjuration Oath.

At this period Sir Robert Grierson appears to
have been acting with the authority of Steward of
Kirkcudbright. So great was his reputation among
the gentlemen of the district for capacity as a man
of business, and activity in the performance of
public duty, that Maxwell, Earl of Nithsdale,
a Roman Catholic, formally ' disponed' to Sir
Robert Grierson the office of Steward of Kirkcudbright, hereditary in the Nithsdale family, during
the minority of his son. The young earl was
only of the age of seven when he succeeded his
father, who had directed that Sir Robert should
hold the Stewardship ' Aye and whill [until] he
[the young Maxwell] be fourtein years of age,' as
it is quaintly expressed in the original bond.[1]

---

[1] Robert Maxwell, fourth Earl of Nithsdale, had a commission
from ' the Committee on Church affairs' to apprehend those
concerned in the rebellion, and to prevent conventicles. He

The increased severity of the Privy Council in
the early part of 1685 was considered to be
necessary on account of the boldness of the
Cameronian body in publishing their 'Apologetical
Declaration,' the utterance of Renwick, their fanatic
leader. As the small body of Presbyterians who
so rashly declared their opinions and intentions
(especially with regard to 'viperous and malicious
Bishops and Curates') in that paper; and affixed
it upon a 'competent number of market crosses,'
were chiefly to be found in the south-western
counties of Scotland, these districts suffered most
heavily in the measures of repression taken by
the Government. One of the sections of Wodrow's
History deals especially with 'The Persecution
this year on the score of the society's (that is the
Cameronian) Declaration.' It is added that at
this time 'the Fury of the Parties as they went up
and down seeking their prey was unparalleled.'

The consequence of this Declaration was the

married Lady Lucie Douglas. Their son William, fifth and
last earl, was born in 1676. A copy of the 'backbond,'
granted by Sir Robert Grierson about 1685, in favour of Lady
Mary Maxwell, daughter of the fourth earl, is preserved at
Terregles.—*Book of Caerlaverock*, i. 414. William, fifth Lord
Nithsdale, married Lady Winifred Herbert, the heroine of the
romantic story of her husband's escape from the Tower.

'Abjuration Oath.' Those taking it were entitled
to a certificate of loyalty, as they stated that they
abhorred and disowned the treasonous document.
But the oath was the cause of much suffering.
The activity of Colonel Douglas[1] and the Laird of
Lag was fully taxed in the endeavour to press this
new Test upon the people. The Privy Council's
instructions were that all persons, whether with
arms or not, refusing to disown the Declaration
upon oath, were to be immediately put to death
provided there were two witnesses.

In February of this year King Charles ii. died,
and was succeeded in the rule of these kingdoms
by his brother, the Duke of York.

During the reign of Charles, the Duke of
Queensberry had been in the highest favour with
the king. He had held the most dignified offices,[2]
although he was understood to be a man of no

[1] The Hon. James Douglas, brother of the Duke of Queensberry
and of Lady Henrietta Grierson, was a member of the Faculty of
Advocates, afterwards Colonel of the Guards in Scotland. He
attained the rank of Lieut.-General, and died at Namur in 1691.

[2] William, third Earl of Queensberry, was appointed Justice-
General of Scotland, 1st June 1680; Extraordinary Lord of
Session, 1681; Marquis, 1682; Duke, 1684; and President of
the Council to James vii., of which office he was deprived.
Concurring with the Revolution, he was a second time appointed
a Lord of Session. He died at Edinburgh in March 1695.

attainment in point of education, but endowed with much natural intelligence. As High Treasurer in the latter part of Charles's reign he was the chief power in Scotland. There is reason to believe that Sir Robert Grierson, throughout the greater part of his public career, was in most respects in accord with his brother-in-law, the Duke of Queensberry, whose sentiments with regard to the Presbyterian party were of the bitterest description; and it was no doubt to some extent in consequence of a feeling of responsibility for the state of their own districts, that the measures of repression in those parts, carried out by Sir Robert Grierson, were characterised by extreme severity.

The bearing of King James at his coronation gave no assurance of his wish to maintain the Protestant religion. And the increased rigour of the measures against the Presbyterians was considered to justify the idea that the struggle they had now to carry on was one directly against the abominations of Popery, synonymous in their minds with a combination of all the powers of darkness. The quaint and pungent passage which heads this section of the narrative, is from the writings of Master Alexander Sheilds, one of the most violent of the followers of Renwick, who afterwards served as chaplain to the Cameronian Regiment. It is no more than an expression of the feeling with which the Covenanting mind was imbued at this time.

Now, it was thought, that thing had come to pass foreshadowed in what many singular, self-denied, and solid Christians had seen, as testified by godly Mr. John Blackader and others ; how, in a desert place in Stirlingshire, was seen the brae-side covered with the appearance, as it were, of men and women singing with heavenly voices, the 121st Psalm,—' I to the hills will lift mine eyes ;' with a milk-white horse, and a blood-red saddle on his back, standing in the midst of the people. The white horse and the blood-red saddle were now accounted for—as a child could not fail to under-stand—by the torrent of tyranny and oppression which threatened to sweep away all trace of Gospel truth in what was styled the ' Spate of Persecution.'

Lord Macaulay, in his *History*, cites the pro-ceedings of a single fortnight in the early part of this year as illustrative of ' the crimes which goaded the peasantry of the western Lowlands into mad-ness.' It was during this period that Lag figured most prominently. In February 1685 occurred one of the two cases which have, more than all the rest, served to stamp a mark upon his memory.

On the 11th February 1685, it appears Captain Bruce of Earlshall, the colleague and lieutenant of Claverhouse, and one of the most zealous officers in the cause, captured a party of six Covenanters at Lochenkeit, in the parish of Kirkpatrick-Durham, of whom four were summarily disposed of. The other two, Edward Gordon and Alexander MacCubbin of Glencairn, were carried by Captain Bruce before Lag, who was actively pressing the Abjuration Oath upon the people in the neighbourhood of the Bridge of Urr. His wish was to pronounce instant sentence upon the prisoners, but they were allowed a day's grace, at the intercession of Earlshall, who thought an assize should be called for their trial. At first Lag 'swore bloodily that he would seek no assizes,' but the Captain got the matter put off till the morrow, when he and ' monsterous Lag,' without any trial, ' caused hang them on a growing tree¹ near the kirk of Irongray,' MacCubbin having sent a pious message to his

---

¹ On an occasion somewhat similar, one hundred years before, the following couplet had been written and set up :—

' Cresce diu felix Arbor, semperque vireto
O, utinam, semper talia poma feras.'

The tree at Irongray, however, it is said, never bore a leaf again. It formed part of a clump of oaks on a knoll near where the men were buried. ' Immediately beyond these trees is the

wife, to the effect that he 'left her and the two babes upon the Lord, and to His promise.'

The hangman asked his forgiveness ; he replied, ' Poor man, I forgive thee, and all men ; thou hast a miserable calling upon earth.' They both died, it is added, 'with much composure and cheerfulness.'

The second incident alluded to is that of the death of John Bell of Whiteside, and of 'four others with him.' As the narrative shows, ' it deserves a room here, as what is due to the memory of a good man.' The case is remarkable inasmuch as the chief sufferer was of a different class from that of the majority of those who suffered the penalty of death at this time. He is described as the only son of the heiress of Whiteside,[1] in the

farm-house of Hallhill, formerly a mansion-house. It is said the lady of the Hallhill, or Haughill, gave her scarf to bind the eyes of Gordon and MacCubbin, for which she was condemned to seven years' banishment to the colonies. When near the coast of Virginia a violent storm broke the vessel in pieces, and she escaped by floating to the shore on a cask ; and lived to return to Scotland at the Revolution.'

[1] The lands of Caldside and Whyteside had come to the Bell family by charter dated 3d May 1534. The widow of John Bell of Whyteside, Marion, daughter of M'Culloch of Ardwell, married Alexander, fifth Viscount Kenmure. Her son, John Bell, had succeeded to the estate of Whyteside in 1682.— M'Kerlie's *Lands and their Owners in Galloway.*

parish of Anwoth, who, after his father's death, had married the Viscount Kenmure, one of the 'disaffected.'

He is said to have been a man of piety and sagacity, and to have borne, since the battle of Bothwell Bridge, 'a sore Fight of Tribulations.' Immediately after the battle, as might have been expected, Bell's house was plundered by the king's troops. Two years afterwards Claverhouse and a detachment of his men lay several weeks in the house, they with their horses 'eating up all his medows,' until they had devoured everything but a flock of sheep, which they drove away with them on their departure. What they could not carry away with them, 'they sold to the people for Meat and Drink, yea, they broke down the very Timber of the House and burnt it. Claverhouse took upon him, without any Warrant that I can observe, to gift his whole crop to the curate,'[1]—so the narrative runs. This may have been considered fair treatment for a defeated rebel, but the manner of his death is a tragedy of exceeding blackness.

There are several traditional stories of the narrow escapes of John Bell while he was a

[1] Wodrow's *Sufferings of the Church*.

wanderer on the hills.   His last fatal adventure is
told somewhat in this fashion in Galloway.

In February 1685 Lag, with a party of Claverhouse's horse and Strachan's dragoons, were on
their way from Wigtown to Dumfries. After
passing Gatehouse-of-Fleet in the afternoon, their
route lay across a dreary waste, which they en-
livened, as was their wont, with song and joke.
But by the time they had entered on Irelandton
Muir, a dense fog had rolled up from the Borgue
shore of the Solway.   Night was coming on.
Therefore Lag called a halt, and proposed to send
back for a guide.   One of the troopers, however,
said he could discern a light some way to the left.
They spurred on, and arrived at the house, namely
the mailing of old Gabriel Rain, at Gordon-Cairn.
He and his aged wife were the only inmates, a
feckless old couple.   Hearing the tramp of horses,
he hospitably stirred up the fire and went to the
door.   He was met by Lag, who demanded if they ◌
were on the right road for Dumfries.

'Na, gentlemen,' said the old man, 'ye're clean
aff the road, but ye'll won on't again, gin ye haud
weel to the knowe-tap doon bye, syne turn to
your ——— '

'We want more than directions,' cried Lag;

'we've wasted too much time already on your cursed muir. Come on, and show the road.'

Gabriel objects that he is an old man and frail.

'Put the auld carle up behind you,' he said to a trooper; 'if he will not walk, he shall ride.'

Gabriel preferred to walk; and conducted the party some way, when he, pointing out lights through the fog, said—

'Haud straight for the licht, and five minutes will bring ye to Calfarran farm-house.'

Old Rain had handed the party over to one he knew would be able to deal with them if any could, namely to Thomas Clinton, gudeman of Calfarran, a shrewd man who, like Laurie Lapraik, was thought a 'sly tod,' ready enough 'to hunt wi' the hound, and rin wi' the hare;' for they were not all martyrs.

'Atweel,' said Thomas, 'ye're no aboon a bow-shot aff the road. I'll pit ye on't mysel'; but ye'll hae to gang doon the Spoot o' Auchentalloch, a road I'm no unco fond o' mysel' in the clud o' nicht. But you sodgers,' he added pleasantly, 'hae nae fear o' God or deevil.'

The joke was ill-timed. Sir Robert, rendered suspicious by this alacrity, began to make inquiry about some of the neighbours. Did he happen to know Mayfield?

' Fine,' said Thomas, equally suspicious, ' I ken Mayfield, and the man that's in it; but ye 're far frae Mayfield, and a coarse road it is tae't; ye canna gang there the nicht.'

' Be the way as rough and crooked as the Covenanter's road to heaven, I shall be there this night—and you shall guide us,' said Lag.

Clinton seemed to be nothing loth; and on the way inquired casually if none of the troopers could sing; he had heard they were all fine singers. The hint was a good one; and nothing would serve them but that the ' psalm-singing dog' should first sing himself. Thomas was quite ready to oblige the gentlemen. ' Then give us,' say they, ' *Awa, Whigs, awa* '—

> ' The deil sat grim amang the reek,
>   Thrang bundling brimstane matches;
> And crooned 'mang dour buik-taking Whigs
>   Scraps o' auld Calvin's catches.'

Thus he sang, and it was noticed that as the troop neared the house of Mayfield, the song waxed louder and louder, till the musician could raise his voice no higher. As had been foreseen, on entering the house they found it deserted, the door open,

sticks, bonnets, chairs in confusion on the floor.
Lag was furious—'But for the singing of that
rebel dog we should have had them.' But they
had compelled him to sing, therefore he was spared
rough treatment.

Here they were obliged to put up for the night.
Thomas knew all about the stables and outhouses
where the horses might best be put up, and was
most active in seeing after the comfort of Sir
Robert and his officers. To make a good fire, he
would fetch a load of peats from the stack—they
saw no more of Clinton, however, or his peats : he
was off, into the mist.

The fugitives fell into the hands of the party
next day, and proved to be John Bell of Whiteside
and his four companions.

Though it was said quarter had been promised
by the men who first seized them, they were ordered
to be shot instantly—

> ' Scarce time did they to them allow
> Befor ther Maker ther knes to bow.'

For, on Bell's asking that they might have a few
minutes' respite for prayer, Lag replied—'What a
devil have you been doing so many years in these
hills—have you not prayed enough?' It is even

said that Lag refused to allow Bell's body to be buried.

Some time after this Kenmure, Claverhouse, and Lag met at Kirkcudbright, when Lord Kenmure upbraided Grierson for his cruelty to one whom he knew to be a gentleman, and nearly related to him ; and especially because burial had been refused for his body. Lag swore at him, and made a most offensive reply: ' Take him,' he cried, ' if you will, and salt him in your beef barrel,' on which the Viscount drew his sword, and would have run him through, had not Claverhouse interfered and separated them.

The inscription on Bell's gravestone at Anwoth is to the effect that quarter had been given by Douglas of Morton. Lag's speech at the death of Bell is also given. The tomb of Robert Lennox of Irelandton, one of Bell's companions in death, is, or was, to be found in the churchyard of Girthon; on it his fate is thus recorded : ' Shot to death by Grier of Lag.' The value of such tombstones as evidence in the cases in question is, of course, slight unless we know the date of the stones ; but they indicate, at any rate, that the stories were current and credited in the neighbourhood, which is all that is meant to be shown at present.

It is recorded as one of the distinguishing features of Lag's dealings with the unfortunate Covenanters who fell into his hands, at this time, that he was invariably deaf to all entreaty on the part of the poor creatures for the briefest space for prayer before they were put to death. It will easily be understood how such useless cruelty would exasperate the country against the author of it, and (even without the fearful image of the horse-shoe ' deep-dinted on the forehead,' which tradition, or Sir Walter Scott, has ascribed to him) render him an object of superstitious terror.

In the narrative of these doings there is a ghastly sameness, unrelieved by a vestige of anything picturesque or any trace of romance. The record of this period is one of grim slaughter, and it is certain that the stern and inflexible method with which the dread machinery of the law was kept agoing by the officers intrusted with the duty, fostered the idea that it was with a certain *gusto*, or a measure of enjoyment, that they personally carried out the behests of a pitiless Government.

One incident in which Lag was concerned has in it something more of dramatic effect and interest.

The narrative is entitled ' A particular vouched Account of a search for a gentleman in the Parish

of Anwoth in Galloway.' Out of a delicate consideration for him, the gentleman is not named,
as he, having been forced to yield afterwards—'a
great grief to him,'—could not be classed with the
martyrs who held out to the death, for conscience'
sake. His house had been searched by Lag's orders,
but the proprietor was missed ; a few days after,
the Laird of Lag and Colonel Douglas with a party
came suddenly down upon the house ; but, again
missing their prey, they proceeded to destroy what
had been overlooked on the former visit, spoiling
what they could not carry off 'for bulk.' They
slit the feather beds and bolsters, and turned out
the feathers, and carried off the ticking, with other
things in the house that were portable ! Again,
on the 7th April, Colonel Douglas and a company
of foot, were equally unsuccessful in their search.
But, it is related, the foot were not a mile off the
house till Lag came down upon it again, with a
party of dragoons, to renew the search for the
gentleman and some others. He brought in all
the neighbours, and swore them under the most
horrid oaths and imprecations, whether they knew
anything of the haunts of the persons he was seeking. Among others, they seized upon the gentleman's daughter, and questioned her regarding her

father's movements, apparently with little success,
till she was suddenly asked where she had been the
night before while they were searching the house.
The young gentlewoman, expecting no hazard
could ensue, answered that she had been at the
house of a lady in the neighbourhood. Lag instantly sent a party to that house; and the result
was that both the gentlewomen were carried off
prisoners.

The next scene in the progress of the search is,
as a 'situation,' highly effective. Lag carries his
prisoners down to the sea-beach, and, while he and
his men *draw* the rocks by the shore, a party of
dragoons are picketed some little way off, 'to
catch any that should be chased out of the caves
about the shore.' The hunt ends in the gentleman
and his companions being unearthed, and in cele-
bration of the happy event the hunters all adjourn
to his house, which they now *perfectly* spoiled;
destroying everything that had not been rendered
useless before.

The male prisoners having been deposited in
Wigtown Jail, and well threatened, were left for
some days to their own thoughts, which could not
have been very agreeable, for, one by one, they
gave in and took the Abjuration Oath; before the

last submitted, however, Lag returned and 'swore terribly that he should be in a few minutes (as he impiously called the future state) *barking and flying.*' It was considered, it is said, 'a mighty piece of lenity' that his life was spared upon his yielding. This narrative is given as an example of what is quaintly defined as the 'imposing spirit of the time.'

Naturally much of the discredit of over-zealous conduct on the part of his subordinates fell upon Sir Robert Grierson. It is undoubted that much barbarity was perpetrated under cover of his name and authority. For example, it is narrated that on one occasion about this time, 'a party of Grier o' Lag's dragoons,' as they are described, met in the south part of the parish of Borgue a poor tailor on his way to work. He bore no more formidable weapons than his needles and ellwand ; but he was closely searched. In those days the tailor, it appears, made the clothes of both male and female, and sewed for the common people, and acted as mantua-maker to the ladies, whose dresses, to be in the mode, had pieces of lead inserted at different points to make them hang as they should. Consequently this poor man was found to have his pockets stored with pieces of lead. He was instantly charged with the intention of casting bullets. It was in vain that he attempted to explain the demands of fashion; and that he was in the employment of ladies in the neighbourhood. The proceedings in his case were very short. The grave of this man at Kirkandrew is said to have occupied much of the attention of 'Old Mortality.'

There can be no question but that Sir Robert Grierson was a man of great ability and wonderful energy; in fact, the most capable man in those parts. This much may be inferred from the amount of public business of all sorts[1] that fell to his share. In private matters also he seems to have been the man to consult with, and to trust in

[1] For example, there is among the public records in the Register House, Edinburgh, a document dated 1st April 1684, of considerable length and much detail, entitled ' A bond anent Irish victual for the Lairds of Lag and Kelburn,' by which Sir Robert Grierson and John Boyle of Kelburn undertake by order of the Privy Council, ' to search for, seize, and apprehend all Irish victuall and cattle, and salt beef made thereof, as shall be imported from Ireland into any harbour, river, etc.' and to burn any boats or vessels, and ' secure the persons of the Skippers; ' and especially they bind themselves that in carrying out these instructions they will not sell any of the ' victuall ' for their own advantage. These instructions were afterwards embodied in an Act of James VII., Parl. 1, cap. 14.

emergencies. On such occasions, it is but fair to
say—and it is refreshing to have to record it—he
seems to have acted well and justly. For instance,
when he assumed the office of Steward of Kirkcudbright 'disponed' to him by the Earl of Nithsdale
during his young son's minority, as already
mentioned, it is stated that he was far from seeking to benefit himself by his tenure of the office,
which he held 'only for the promotion of the
king's service.' Amongst other details connected
with this, it was arranged that 'the whole of the
lardner mart' should be given to Lady Mary
Maxwell, sister of the young earl, as well as the
half of the profits of the office, the other half
being expended in the payment of the deputies
who performed the duties of it.[1]

Moreover, one of the heaviest charges against
the persecutors in the South-west was that of

[1] After the death of Robert, fourth Earl of Nithsdale, his widow,
Lady Lucie Douglas, got a pension of £200 from Charles II., on
the ground of poverty, and for the maintenance of her son, the
fifth earl, and her daughter, the Lady Mary Maxwell, who
afterwards married Charles, fourth Earl of Traquair. On the
accession of James VII., the young Nithsdale and his mother
petitioned for the continuance of the allowance and for a grant
of 4000 merks, annually, out of the forfeited estates of the
rebels. Only the £200 was given.—*Book of Caerlaverock*, vol. i.
p. 414.

wholesale spoliations at the expense of the sufferers;
but, in this respect at all events, Lag seems to
have been a man of a different stamp from those
sheriffs and deputies against whom such charges
were made, but who—if we may believe Wodrow
—do not seem to have been much the better for
the property thus acquired, for he says that in his
time—'a sensible Moth hath been seen to be in
such ill-got estates.'

The estates of the unfortunate Bell of Whiteside were ' disponed ' to the young Earl of Nithsdale.[1]

In consideration of his services and ' sufferings,'
John Graham of Claverhouse was rewarded with
the estate of Freuch, which Patrick M'Dowall, the
owner, lost by *forfalture* on conviction of rebellion.[2]
It does not appear that any such windfall came
Sir Robert's way. But it is recorded in the
minutes of the Presbytery of Wigtown how ' Sir
Robert Grier of Lagg,' in his capacity of Sheriff,
gave directions to ' set in tack,' or rent, to tenants
several of the forfeited estates of the disaffected,
and was active in recovering the mails and dues of

[1] *Book of Caerlaverock*, vol. i. p. 414.
[2] The Act of Ratification bears date 28th May 1681.—
Hereditary Sheriffs of Galloway, p. 386.

the lands in the Sheriff Court;[1] it is not insinuated that any of these steps were taken with a view to his own gain.

Against Sir James Turner, the commander of the king's forces, there were brought *twenty-one* different charges of extortion in the Stewartry of Kirkcudbright, for which he was brought to account—for alleged 'quartering of sojers;' wrongful 'fining for baptizing by outed Ministers;' fathers fined for their daughters baptizing by outed Ministers, 'though the daughters were *forisfamiliate* [*i.e.* out of the household] six months;' fining 'one that lay a year bed-fast;' 'whole parishes' indiscriminately fined; and so on —to the extent of £30,000.[2] Lag seems to have been innocent of such self-aggrandisement and rapacity.

On the accession of James vii. to the throne, the Duke of Queensberry was continued in his office of High Treasurer of Scotland. Coincident with the occasion of the duke's paying his duty to the new king, Sir Robert had the honour of a Baronetcy of Nova Scotia conferred on him. This

[1] *History Vindicated*, 1867, p. 59.
[2] *Memoirs of his own Life*, by Sir James Turner, Edin., 1829.

was in March 1685. In the course of the memorable interview between the king and his treasurer, Queensberry is reported to have used much plainness of speech, and to have said that if the king 'had any thoughts of changing the established religion he could not make any one step with him in that matter; though he would take care to live as became a loyal and dutiful subject.'[1] James gave the required assurances; and Queensberry was sent as High Commissioner with royal authority to meet the Scottish Parliament, which he did in the end of April.

The speech he made on this occasion was a very remarkable one, and, in accordance with what has been said already of the sympathy in such matters between the brothers-in-law, may be taken to express Lag's views. After speaking of the king's resolution to maintain the government of the Church as by law established, the revenues, and the prerogatives of the Crown, Queensberry concluded with the desire—'that effectual Means might be fallen upon, for destroying that desperate phanatical and irreclaimable Party, who had brought them to the Brink of Ruin and Disgrace, and were no more Rebels against the King, than

[1] Bishop Burnet's *History of his own Time*.

Enemies of Mankind, Wretches of such monstrous Principles and Practices, as past Ages never heard, nor those to come will hardly believe.'[1]

Such were the words addressed to a Parliament prepared to carry compliance with the royal wishes to a point of shameless degradation; and they no doubt express the creed of those intrusted with a task which did not seem a hopeless one; namely, of stamping out a contemptible rebellion. The most objectionable of the measures which marked the early days of James's reign were passed by this Parliament, presided over by Queensberry. The Excise of foreign and inland commodities was handed over to the Crown for ever. Persons refusing to give testimony in cases of treason, field- or house-conventicles, and Church-irregularities, were deemed to have incurred the punishment due to such crimes. Every one owning or concurring in the League and Covenant was considered guilty of treason. Two hundred and sixty thousand pounds annually was voted to the King.

If in all these concessions it was, as was thought, the Duke of Queensberry's object to exalt the royal prerogative, and so recommend himself to the King, he was much mistaken. Bishop Burnet

[1] Crawfurd's *Lives of Officers of State*, Edin., 1726.

says, 'he soon found he had deceived himself in thinking that anything but the delivering up of his religion would be acceptable long. And he saw, after he had prepared a cruel scheme of Government, other men were trusted with the management of it.' For a little while there was a lull in the fury of the Persecution, for the excellent reason—as one writer gives it—that there seemed to be few left who were worth persecuting.

Though the catalogue of Lag's misdeeds is not exhausted, still, lest the reader's patience should be, mention will only be made of the case which has, more than any other in the history of this period, brought the name of Sir Robert Grierson into notoriety. In any sketch of his career it cannot be passed over without attention. This is the case of the *Wigtown Martyrs*, as it is styled. It is one of those instances of cruelty of the terrible fortnight in May 1685, spoken of by Lord Macaulay. It has been the subject of much discussion.

GUILTY, OR NOT GUILTY?

Of dolorous deith they doutit not the deir,
    The veritie declaring fervently.
And martyrdome they sufferit paciently ;
    Doctrine and deith war bath acquivalent.

SIR DAVID LINDSAY.

CHAPTER IV.

GUILTY, OR NOT GUILTY?

THE circumstances of this case, as stated by Lord
Macaulay in one of his most picturesque paragraphs,
are as follows :—'On the same day [the 11th of
May 1685], two women, Margaret M'Lachlan
and Margaret Wilson, the former an aged widow,
the latter a maiden of eighteen, suffered death for
their religion in Wigtownshire. They were offered
their lives if they would consent to abjure the
cause of the insurgent Covenanters, and to attend
the Episcopal worship. They refused, and they
were sentenced to be drowned. They were carried
to a spot where the Solway overflows twice a day,
and fastened to stakes fixed in the sand between
high and low water mark. The elder sufferer was
placed near to the advancing flood, in the hope
that her last agonies might terrify the younger
into submission. The sight was dreadful. But

E

the courage of the survivor was sustained by an
enthusiasm as lofty as any that is recorded in
martyrology. She saw the sea draw nearer and
nearer, but gave no sign of alarm. She prayed
and sang verses of psalms till the waves choked her
voice. When she had tasted the bitterness of death,
she was, by a cruel mercy, unbound and restored
to life. When she came to herself, pitying friends
and neighbours implored her to yield. " Dear
Margaret, only say, ' God save the King ! ' " The
poor girl, true to her stern theology, gasped out,
" May God save him, if it be God's will ! " Her
friends crowded round the presiding officer. " She
has said it ; indeed, sir, she has said it ! " " Will
she take the abjuration?" he demanded. "Never!"
she exclaimed ; " I am Christ's—let me go ! " And
the waters closed over her for the last time.' [1]

This graphic paragraph is one of those passages in which the historian gives opportunity
for the critic to hint that the picturesque has been
held more closely in view than perfect accuracy.
In the first place, the context may lead one to infer
that the blame of this transaction was partly due
to John Graham of Claverhouse; whereas it was
David Graham, his brother, who was concerned in

[1] *History*, i. 501.

it. Further, when the historian states that it was 'for their religion' they died, he has evidently overlooked the statement of Wodrow, his authority, regarding the nature of the crime charged ; though no doubt refusal to take the Abjuration Oath, into which the crime of these women ultimately resolved itself, might be construed as a matter of conscience, and so, of religion. Wodrow's words are: 'Brought to their trial before the Laird of Lag ; Colonel David Graham, Sheriff; Major Windram ; Captain Strachan; and Provost Cultrain, who gave all three [a third prisoner was included in the indictment] an indictment for *Rebellion, Bothwell Bridge, Air's Moss*, and being present at twenty field conventicles.'[1]

But a still greater oversight in what should have been an exact history of the case is that, though it is the truth that the women were tried and convicted by the commissioners named, it is equally certain that a reprieve, or respite, was granted by the Privy Council. The commission[2] under which

---

[1] Wodrow's *History*, book iii. c. ix. 506.

[2] The Lords Justices of Wigtownshire under the royal commission of 27th March 1685 were Viscount Kenmure; Sir Robert Grierson of Lag; Sir David Dunbar of Baldoon; Sir Godfrey M'Culloch of Mireton; and Mr. David Graham, Sheriff of Galloway. These were ordained to concur with

the women were tried bears date 27th March 1685;
the trial took place on the 13th April; and the
prisoners were reprieved on the 30th of the same
month, when an absolute pardon was recommended.
The only question for discussion was, and is,—
Were the women drowned?

On this point much contention followed Lord
Macaulay's statement. Amongst others Principal
Tulloch, of St. Andrews University, argued that,
notwithstanding the picturesque embellishments of
the historian's account, the facts were as stated,
though he could not explain how the tragedy
should have ended so, in view of the *reprieve*.[1]

It was held on the other side that no authentic
record of the execution was in existence, the records
of the Burgh of Wigtown being silent on the
subject; that the story chiefly rested on anonymous pamphlets put out after the Revolution,
when it was desired to take a revenge on the Laird
of Lag and his associates; that several writers, who
would have been likely to mention such a case,

Colonel Douglas (brother of the Lord High Commissioner). A
letter of the Privy Council of 29th May, after the alleged
drowning, is addressed to Kenmure and Lag, as the leading
Commissioners for Wigtown and the Stewartry.—*Memorials of
Dundee*, vol. ii. p. 81.

[1] *Macmillan's Magazine*, Dec. 1862.

as Sir George Mackenzie, the Lord Advocate, himself concerned in it, and Lord Fountainhall, alike ignored the whole matter.

At this point Mr. Mark Napier, Sheriff of Dumfriesshire, produced his *Case for the Crown*, in which, among other arguments, he showed how the narrative usually followed had been compiled some twenty-five years after the date of the event, when there had been a call by the General Assembly of the Church of Scotland for details of the late sufferings of the Church which, as now, were thought to be in danger of being forgotten in the tumult of new opinions. It was between 1708 and 1711 that this demand was made, and the record of the Kirk-session of the Parish of Penninghame describing the event bears date 25th February of the latter year.

These facts were so well and cogently urged by Sheriff Napier in his pamphlet that the statement of the fabrication of the evidence by the old Kirk-session, the falsehood of the whole story of the drowning, and the adoption of it by Wodrow were very generally accepted.

In December 1863 a strong article was printed in *Blackwood's Magazine*, the contribution of an English barrister-at-law, in which Macaulay's statement, and any other theory regarding the fate of the martyrs than that contended for by the Sheriff of Dumfriesshire, were shown to be absurd. Not unnaturally, some value was attached to this opinion, as the judgment of an impartial arbitrator, and one accustomed to weigh evidence.

So the matter rested for a while. But though many might be convinced of the soundness of these views, and the exactness of the train of evidence by which they were upheld, there never was the slightest doubt in the minds of the people down in Wigtownshire as to this matter. The facts had been passed down to them by the surest hands. If they had not seen the execution themselves, they knew who had.

Thus old Miss Susan Heron, who lived long in Wigtown, and died in 1834,[1] used to repeat the words of her grandfather, which she had heard from his own lips—and he had been present at the execution of the women—' There were cluds o' folk on the Sands that day in clusters here and

---

[1] In Penninghame Churchyard, the family tombstones show that this venerable lady must have been eleven years of age when her grandfather died in 1758, at the age of ninety-four.— *Hereditary Sheriffs of Galloway*, p. 431.

there, praying for the women as they were put down.'[1]

And there were legends which these good people could not cast out from their belief. 'Legend and Song,' it is allowed, 'are never judicial, but work with strong lights and shadows.' Thus, years after the affair at Blednoch had become a picturesque and melancholy incident of the past, a down-broken old man used to be seen wandering alone. He, by the will of Heaven, was afflicted with an intolerable and unquenchable thirst, insomuch that he never durst venture abroad without carrying along with him a large jar full of water; so cruel was his unnatural appetite. As he crawled along with his extraordinary load, people would pass him by with silent horror. They knew the cause of his disease. This man had been the Town Officer of Wigtown, who, when the younger sufferer was raised out of the water, and refused to save her life by uttering the few words that would have sufficed, thrust her down with his halbert, saying,—' Tak anither drink, hinny ;' and bidding her ' clep wi' the partons,' *i.e.* gossip with the crabs.[2]

[1] *Hereditary Sheriffs of Galloway*, p. 431.
[2] A young gentleman from Edinburgh, on a visit to these

But the arguments were not yet closed, nor the cause ripe for final judgment.

Though the burgh records were bare of any information regarding the fate of these people, it was by no means the case that the records of the Church Courts were equally silent. On the contrary, it was found that when the call for authentic information on the subject of the recent sufferings was made, that is, about 1708, a graphic statement was drawn up by the Kirk-sessions of the parishes concerned, not hurriedly, but with, apparently, great deliberation; and passed up to the higher Courts for approval or criticism. A charge has been made against the persons who framed these narratives, of deliberate falsehood and fabrication.

But on inquiry it appeared that the original compilers of the statement were ministers of good repute; several of whom, it seemed, had been established in the districts concerned at the date of the occurrence. Among the elders were included many men of substance, and county gentlemen of

parts, and full of the latest theories current in the capital regarding the martyrs, on one occasion had explained at some length to a resident of the neighbourhood how modern inquiry had shown that it was improbable, not to say impossible, that the execution could have taken place, replied, 'I dar say, Mr. Dauvid, it may be a' as ye say—but *the wemen were drooned!*'

good position, of an age to justify the idea that they had personal knowledge of the events they reported.

Many other items of proof were put together till a goodly mass of affirmative evidence was the result. For instance, after nineteen years of grief of heart for his share in the transaction in question, one man is recorded to have prayed of the Presbytery the comfort of Church privileges, of which he had been deprived; and, strangely, one of the elders of whom he made the request was Provost Coltran,[1] a prime mover in the trial, though erroneously supposed to have been concerned in the execution. This, it was urged, would have been absurd, had there been no execution. But more curiously still, a pamphlet[2] of 1703, by an Episcopal writer, was found, in which, while excusing something else, the remarkable phrase was used

[1] William Coltran of Drummoral was likewise Sheriff-Substitute of Wigtown, while David Graham was Sheriff. He was Commissioner to the Parliament, and a Member of the famous Convention of Estates of 1689, that declared the throne to be vacant.—*Hereditary Sheriffs of Galloway*, p. 441. He died in 1708, and it is understood that his son, Patrick, was awarded the sum of £25 in 1711 on account of his father's services towards the Union.

[2] *A short Character of the Presbyterian spirit in so far as it can be gathered out of their own books*, etc., 1703.

with reference to the affair at Blednoch—' *drowned indeed they were.*'   This pamphlet, it appears, was printed by Andrew Symson, the former Episcopal clergyman of Wigtown, who had marked Margaret Lauchlison as 'disorderly' on the list of the persons of his parish, and was written by his son, an unwilling witness.   What reply—if any—this bit of evidence called forth, I have not been able to ascertain.

Moreover, it was shown that Thomas Wilson, brother of the younger sufferer, who was sixteen at the time of the tragedy, was still in the parish of Penninghame when the Session record was drawn up, that is, in 1711 ; a decent, worthy man, who had frequently been asked to accept office as an elder.   Many years after the publication of Wodrow's *History* this man was living to testify to its accuracy on this point.

Such was the nature of the new evidence.   In due course there was a reply, in which it was understood no new facts were brought forward.

Still it was contended that the Martyr's gravestone, and its inscription, recording in rough verse the fate of Margaret Wilson, and that—

> ' The actors of this cruel crime
> Was Lagg, Strachan, Winram, and Graham,'

were apocryphal in character; that no record or notice whatever exists regarding the obsequies of these pseudo-martyrs; that similar monuments have been set up in our own time at different places, on no evidence.

With regard to the pamphlet, *Popery Reviving,* 1714, which had turned up at a late stage of the discussion, and was mentioned as casting light on the *mode* of the execution, it was contended that Wodrow, though he knew of the book, writing in 1722, stuck to his own account, which cannot be reconciled with that in the pamphlet.

Never had a controversy been better, or more skilfully, fought out than this between the Rev. Archibald Stewart, minister of Glasserton (assisted by the Rev. Thomas Gordon of Newbattle), and Mr. Mark Napier. In the passage of arms many a delicate lunge, and many a slashing blow passed between the combatants. It was pretty to see them. It is not likely that anything of importance will now be added to the record of evidence, so that a verdict may now be fairly come to by any one who is inclined to sit in judgment on Grierson and his companions.

But, to render the subject complete, and, for the reader's assistance in forming an opinion, a note may perhaps be added.

It happened that, during the course of this discussion, Dr. Hill Burton, Historiographer, was engaged upon his *History of Scotland*. It was his duty to watch the case impartially in the interest of the public and of posterity. His remarks are therefore worthy of attention. The seventh volume of his *History*, dealing with the year 1685, appeared in 1870. Having studied such of the pamphlets on both sides of the question as had then been issued, he added a foot-note to his text —'Hence the end of the controversy is to bring us back to Wodrow's conclusion, who says that the recommendation for a remission should have been dealt with as a virtual pardon, so that the people of Wigtown [namely Lag and his colleagues] are deeply guilty, and had no powers for what they did, and the death of these persons was what the Council ought to have prosecuted them for.'[1] Some new discovery of evidence, the historian thought, would be necessary to alter this opinion.

But before the sheets of his seventh volume were printed off, Mr. Mark Napier's second edition, *History Rescued*, was announced, when Dr. Hill Burton was forced to add another foot-note:—'Of course,' he writes,[2] 'this had to be read before

[1] Burton's *Hist. of Scotland*, vol. vii., 1st ed., p. 549.   [2] *Ibid.*

final correction, that it might be seen whether it contained any new and unsuspected discovery.' He does not appear to think it did, and concludes— 'If it be made clear that certain persons are sentenced to death, it will be a natural sequel that the sentence was executed. Nor will it be easy to see why such a sentence was passed, if it can be proved that there was no intention to carry it into execution.' It may be added that Mr. Paget's article in *Blackwood's Magazine*, already noticed, written in 1863, when the discussion was in its infancy, was reproduced in a volume of collected papers by the same author in 1874; but no notice was taken of the final stages of the argument, nor of the new evidence, thus leaving it of little, or no value as an opinion.

AFTER THE STORM.

Antichrist hath not only been revealed and his Kingdom come to its height, but it is clear this day that it is on the falling hand, and his ruin now begun : upon which account we may say ; yea, have cause to sing, that the Winter is past and the Fig Tree putteth forth her leaves that showeth the Sommer's approach. Yea, the singing of birds is heard in our land : let us go forth and meet Him who is now gone out as a mighty man for the Salvation of his Church.

FULFILLING THE SCRIPTURE.

CHAPTER V.

THOUGH the extreme of complaisance had been shown by the Scottish Parliament of James VII. on his accession to the throne, a few nobles had stopped short of absolute servility. The Duke of Queensberry declined to concur in the proposed measures for dealing with the laws against Popery. Though President of the Council, and the holder of other high offices, he withstood James's wishes, and was deprived of his dignities.

It is far from being to his dishonour that the Duke of Queensberry, from holding the position of a dictator in Scotland, sank for the moment into comparative obscurity, and had cause to learn the force of the axiom—

> ‘ Sudden and hie advancements frequentlie
> By precipitous downfall followed be.’

Or, as the same truth—shortly to be impressed on

F

.others in the highest sphere—had been expressed by a noble French author—'La montée aux prospérités est de verre, la cîme tremblement, et la descente un précipice.'

A design was laid to ruin him,[1] which only caution and circumspection frustrated. As Sir Robert Grierson seems to have been at one with his brother-in-law in public matters, it is most probable that he agreed with him at this juncture also.

Besides his Baronetcy, the Laird of Lag received for his services to King James a pension of two hundred pounds a year; which, however, he did not long enjoy.   Suddenly he found his occupation and his pension gone when his royal master was forced to fly from his kingdom, escaping in a fishing smack, to seek safety where he might.

The first news of the end of the Stuart dynasty was the signal for an outburst of anti-Popish rage. In Edinburgh Popes were publicly burned amidst shouts for a free Parliament.   Holyrood was stormed and sacked, and its objectionable contents burned in the High Street.   The contagion instantly spread to Nithsdale and Clydesdale, the stronghold of Popery.   At Dumfries, on Christmas Day, the

[1] Bishop Burnet's *History of His own Time.*

populace made a fierce and turbulent anti-Romanist
demonstration ; and, as at the capital, they collected, for destruction, from the neighbourhood all
the Popish vestments, imagery, books and beads
they could lay their hands on. It became the first
object of the reconstructed Privy Council to see
that all trace of the ancient religion was swept
speedily away. There was no hope of peace till
this were done. It was the duty of the Council
at this stage to intrust the execution of their
orders to the most capable officers throughout
the country ; thus the services of Lag as a diligent
magistrate were again in request.

After the gloomy scenes through which our hero
has been traced, it is a relief to find him engaged
on a duty which has less of the tragic element
in it.

Shortly before his fall King James had been
more than ordinarily active in forcing Roman
Catholics into offices of importance ; as is seen in
his interference in the appointment of a Provost
of Dumfries, the election to which post had been
hitherto in the hands of the town's-people.

For long they were forbidden to elect *any*
Provost ; ultimately they had one, by the king's
order, appointed for them, in the person of the

Laird of Barncleugh, a Roman Catholic gentleman of good standing. Like Mrs. Provost Crosbie, in *Redgauntlet*, he was 'born a Maxwell,'[1] and so 'allied to all the best families in the county.' He seems to have succeeded in ingratiating himself, by means of lavish expenditure, with the people of a town that has ever been famed for appreciation of good eating and drinking. So pleased were they with the compliment of this gentleman coming to live among them, and with his hospitality, that the Town Council voted him 'pipes of wine and sums of money' for his 'encouragement' in such a course. These fine times did not last long, however. The blow suddenly fell which ended the reign of Barncleugh and of the king. During the commotions which ensued, Provost Maxwell disappeared—in some sort of masquerade costume, it was said; but was subsequently made prisoner, about the same time that the detested Earl of Perth was captured in a similar disguise. Instructions were asked of the new Privy Council

[1] Maxwell of Barncleugh was served heir to his grandfather in 1665, and was nominated Provost of Dumfries in 1686. He married Margaret, daughter of John Irving of Friars' Carse, Provost of Dumfries, and Elizabeth Crichton, his wife, daughter of Sir Robert Crichton, who was a brother of the Earl of Dumfries.—*Book of Caerlaverock*, i. 502.

concerning him, which being in due course received were found to be most explicit.

They were read by the Town Council on the 26th December, the day after the riot, and consisted of a letter from the Marquess of Athole, President of the Council, in which, after thanks to the town authorities for their prudent management at this ' dangerous juncture,' the following careful directions were given :—' Detaine as prisoners in your tolbuith thos persones apprehended on this account, except the Laird of Barncleugh your late proveist, who is to be sent hither prisoner by the gentry of your shire, by order of the Laird of Lag and others who have the Counsell's former commands anent him ; and the Counsell doe heirby give order and warrant to Lag and Closeburn or any two of your Towne Counsell to sight what is in the said Barncleugh's cloak-bag, found with him for his disguise ; and to delyver to him such papers therein as properly belong to himselfe, and such as pertaine to your toune to you, and such as belong to the public to be sent under your sealls to the clerk of Counsell.' [1]

We can imagine the amount of gossip and

[1] Town Council Minutes ; M'Dowall's *Hist. of Dumfries*.

'diversion' that this strange turn in the course of events would cause among the worthy citizens; as also the excellent joke that the 'sighting of Barncleugh's cloak-bag,' by Lag and Closeburn, would be considered. We can figure the old Dumfriesians crowding out at the head of the Friars' Vennel to witness the departure of Barncleugh from the Tolbuith, a prisoner for Edinburgh, under the superintendence of the ex-persecutor.

The meeting of Estates was fixed for the fourteenth of March, and it was speedily seen that political morality was exceedingly lax in Scotland. Men of weight were determined that their weight should tell to their own advantage. Self-seeking and time-serving were carried to the most shameful lengths. In the month of April the Duke of Queensberry arrived, and exerted by his presence in the Convention a wholesome influence; his character was fair by comparison with those around him. Though an adherent of James, he had been firm in the Protestant cause, and was still true to hereditary right.

Notwithstanding, as was said by 'a noble writer, much in the secret of things,' the Duke of Queensberry 'was, at the time of the Revolution, sincerely

in the interests of King James;'[1] when the change
became inevitable his Grace declared his views in
a speech to the Convention of Estates,—'that
though he was not fully convinced of their right
in declaring the Throne vacant, yet, since it was
done, he acquiesced; and none deserved it so well
as the Prince and Princess of Orange,' a speech
that was effective in allaying the storm that had
arisen.[2]

But although Sir Robert Grierson seems to have
followed his noble relative thus far in public affairs,
it is certain that he appears henceforth in a
character entirely his own.

The Duke of Queensberry again took a prominent position, and was restored to some of his
former offices.'[3] Lag might also, doubtless, have
benefited by the turn events were taking had he
chosen to conform himself to the new *régime*, and

---

[1] *Account of the Affairs of Scotland relating to the Revolution*,
by the Earl of ——, p. 79, quoted by Crawfurd.

[2] *Ibid.* p. 83.

[3] The Duke of Queensberry was reappointed an extraordinary Lord of Session; at the same time that—on a Sunday
morning in June—fifteen gentlemen were installed as the regular
judges under the new rule. David Home, Lord Crossrig, has
related how it was almost without himself being consulted that
he found he had been included in the number.—Chambers's
Domestic Annals, vol. iii. p. 10.

accepted William as his king. But he preferred to stand aloof, hoping against hope for a restoration, and stoutly refused to take the oath of allegiance and submission. He might have done so without discredit, and without much curtailing his liberty of action. Hamilton, the President of the Convention, had been a Privy Councillor of King James. Athole, the favourite of the Jacobites, had turned servilely to the side of the Prince of Orange, had been snubbed, and again gone back to his party; and so with many others.

In the infamous 'Club' now formed, composed of men disappointed in their aims of personal advancement, were some who, like Sir James Montgomery of Skelmorlie, Annandale, and Ross, had been suffering Covenanters, but now, ulcerated at heart through spite and disappointment, and henceforth dishonest malcontents, were doing their utmost to annoy the Government.

'In one short year these men had been Williamites and violent Jacobites, and became Williamites again,'¹ just as their self-interest seemed to dictate. Ultimately, in their wretched extremity, they were found accusing and informing against one another, in the hope of escaping punishment. Truly 'a

¹ Lord Macaulay.

man's own safety is a god that sometimes makes very grim demands.'

By comparison with such men as these, Lag shines as an honest, declared rebel, an avowed opponent of King William and the Hanoverian line.

Though he began fairly well, it was but an uphill work. The stout and zealous heart was wanting. He knew not, as we do now, that the Hanoverian rule was founded on a rock, from which no power could shake it; but he looked, as many did, wistfully for any opening which might occur to realise his hopes; and so he was led into temptation, and defections from his newly assumed duty under the Whig rule. It was hard to keep up appearances in those days; an unguarded phrase after supper, or an ambiguous toast, was enough to draw attention upon the unwary Jacobite.

A very short time had elapsed when Sir Robert's zeal for his exiled master—whose letter, ' obstinate, cruel, and insolent,' to the Convention had no effect in shaking his loyalty—began to be apparent. He was considered to be a dangerous person, and accordingly classed among the ' suspect.'

It would have been hard for the witnesses to the Truth to believe that such spiritual wickedness as was charged upon him should go without its reward in this life. And indeed there was a Nemesis in wait for Lag ; and retribution in store for him, such as would go some way to satisfy the expectations of the Cameronian faith in respect of special providences.

There is on record a bond [1] dated in the quaint manner which has been long a puzzle to the uninitiated, namely, the 'fyft day of May, Jaj vic four scoir nyne years' (May 5, 1689), by which James Stewart of Castle Stewart, under penalty of five hundred pounds sterling, binds himself that Sir Robert Grierson of Lagg shall—'live peaceably and with all submission to the present Government under King William and Queen Mary,' and shall 'compeire and sigt himself before the Estates of Parliament,' when called on.

The Revolution was not quite six months old when certain nobles and gentlemen well disposed towards the Government conceived the idea of raising troops of horse, with which they should proceed to those districts where it was understood the disaffected were exercising influence. Among these leaders were the Earl of Annandale, Lord Kenmure, and the Earl of Eglintoun. We may hope

[1] Original in the Historical Department, Register House, Edinburgh.

it was not with any memory in his mind of the fate of John Bell, his relative; but so zealous was Lord Kenmure in this service, that, a week before the others could get under way, he had gone off 'at his own hand' (21st May 1689), and seized Sir Robert Grierson in his house, and taken him a prisoner to the Tolbooth at Kirkcudbright, notwithstanding that the day preceding Lag had gone to the Earl of Annandale and declared himself 'weel affected to the Government.'

Sir Robert having lain some time in the Tolbooth of Edinburgh, petitioned the Lords of the Council, who were pleased to order his release on a large bail for his appearance when called upon.[1] This was the beginning of a period of very real hardship and suffering which now came upon Sir Robert Grierson, in which people were not slow to see the hand of a just Providence.

Under date the fifth day of June, Dalrymple writes—'All the malignants for fear are come into the Club; and they all vote alike.' Still Sir Robert held out undauntedly. There is further evidence of his opposition.

[1] MS. Notes by Dr. Robert Chambers from Privy Council Records.

The gallant and chivalrous defence of Edinburgh
Castle, in the hopeless cause of James VII., by the
Duke of Gordon and a handful of determined
men, and the incident of Claverhouse—as he ' rode
straight off' on his way to the North—climbing
the Castle rock to hold an interview with the noble
governor, are of those picturesque bits which
stand out on the page of history, and are never
likely to be forgotten.

On the 14th June 1689, the garrison, after
starving wretchedly on a little oatmeal and putrid
water, yielded to famine. Though borne down
by toil, starvation, and sickness, when they marched
out they were met with the grossest ill-treatment
at the hands of a Presbyterian mob. The Duke
of Gordon retired a prisoner to his own house in
Blair's Close, near the Castle-Hill. Within three
weeks of this date we meet with Lag again.

On the 6th of July an 'information' of a very
pressing description was forwarded to the Duke of
Hamilton, President of the Convention Parliament,
regarding 'a plot' which the person reporting the
matter entreated might be looked into without a
moment's delay. Thus he stated his facts—'This
night about six a cloack I was informed of some
evill inclyned persones who certanely designes some

wicked interprise; what it is I know not, but the particular persons are these belonging to the Castle . . . by ane subscryved paper which some of them hes, there are one Collonell Wilsone, Butler and Dumbar, and some others of English and Irish Officers lurking in toune in Blackfrier wynd, lykewayes Captaine Douglas, Kellhead's brother, Lies, Pringle, and severall others I am surely informed of, which I thought it my duetie in conscience to acquaint your Grace with, that by the Lord's providence their pernicious designe may be frustrat by tymely preventing them.'

It seems that the Duke's informant had been suspiciously well up in the facts of the case, for he adds,—'I wes almost engadged myselfe, which makes me know the truth . . . and shall ever pray for the true Protestant religion.' [1]

Then follows a list of 'Persons apprehended,' some thirty-six of them in all. There were among the prisoners John Maxwell, Barnbauchley; Captain James Wauchope; Lieut-Col. Wilson; Sir Alexander Burnet; Innes of Ortoun; Captain Douglas; Robert Dunbar; [2] Edward Butler; as

---

[1] *Acts of Scots Parliament*, vol. ix. p. 13, App.

[2] This was probably the gallant ship-captain, an expert gunner, who, during the siege, left his wife and children to the

also the Duke of Gordon; Earl of Hume; Viscount Oxenfoord; Captain Ramsay; the Laird of Lag; George Winrahm; 'and some meaner people.'

The peril in which these Jacobite gentlemen found themselves placed by this act of treachery was no imaginary one. There might have come of it more than the heavy imprisonment which fell to the share of Lag, and one or two others of the more inveterate opponents of the Government. The particulars of this case are very precisely given in a letter written by the Duke of Hamilton to Lord Melville, now Secretary of State to King William, but some four years previously a 'fugitated rebel' on the other side. Thus the narrative runs:—

'HOLYROOD-HOUSE, 9th July 1689.

'. . . . On Saturday last, about 11 at night a paper was drapt neir one of the Sentries direct[ed] to me. The sentrie sent it to his officer and he to the Brigadier Balfour, so it was one in the morning before it was brought to me. So soon as I read it

mercy of the people, and offered his services to work the Duke of Gordon's artillery in the Castle.—See *Memorials of Edinburgh Castle*, by James Grant.

and seeing the consequence, I thought there was
no delay to be in the matter, so I imediatly made
the officers gett togither als many of the souldiers
as they could without beating drumes.   I also sent
to the Provest and Magistrats of the toune and
ordered them to secure the ports that none gote
out or in but whom they knew; and then com-
manded a search to be made thorrow all the toune,
and particularly for those persones named in the
peaper found directed to me . . . and it succeeded
so well that most of the persones are taken that
are mentioned in the peaper besides many others
that are suspected to have been on the designe,
and who were discovered to us by one Scott who
has confessed all he knowes ; (this Scott the gold-
smith's sone whoes mother Earl Lithgow maryed)
. . . and Wilson the cheife man he confest to me
before he went to the Castle a great dale more
then what you will see in the letter from thence ;
and particularly that he was at Cranstoune last
week with the Lord Oxfoord [Oxenfoord ?] and
Captain Ramsay, when were present the Earl of
Lauderdale and Lord Maitland . . . with one
John Hay (who lately came from Dundie), brother-
in-law to the said Lord Oxfoord, who and Capt.
Ramsay are now prisoners; and Lauderdale and

his sones are sent for. We have been ever since the search busie at Counsill in the examination of this matter, and has the Parliaments allowance to use torture . . . We think this matter is deeper laid then we have yet discovered, and that Wilson can discover all; and if he does not confess freely it is like he may get the boots or thumbikins.'[1]

All those named were known to be more or less disaffected towards the Revolution Government, and only three days before, namely, on the 3d of July, a list had been drawn out of those members of the Parliament who, despite a proclamation on the subject, had failed to appear for the performance of their duty, ' not being minors, excused, residing without the kingdom, or denounced as papists.' The names of more than one of the gentlemen above-mentioned appear on this return.

The startling information given to the Duke of Hamilton, as we read it, seems to have been well

[1] *Leven and Melville Papers*, Bannatyne Club, pp. 149-50. At this same period Mr. Gilbert Elliot writes to Lord Melville :— ' The morrow the Councell have resolved to examine Liewtennant Collonell Wilson by torture.'—p. 129. A few days after Sir John Dalrymple (afterwards Earl of Stair) announces— ' We have [by] proclamation, put £20,000 *Sterling* on *Dundie's bead;* which may probably *catch him* who must be in the power of the Clans.'—*Mems. of Dundee,* iii. 612.

calculated to arouse apprehension of a formidable conspiracy against the Government or Estates of Parliament. In the end it did not, however, attain great proportions. The object of the combination seems to have been connected with arrangements regarding the avowedly hostile force gathering under Claverhouse. Dr. Hill Burton, who makes very slight mention of this incident, remarks that the Duke of Hamilton, by his vigorous measures, did not escape the suspicion of having exaggerated the danger for party purposes; by inducing an excitement that might be useful as a distraction, seeing things were not going to his mind.[1] Be this as it may, a very few hours after the discovery of the paper, Lag and others of the party found themselves clapped up in the Tolbooth, the ancient prison of Edinburgh.[2]

The imprisonment to which these gentlemen were subjected was no child's-play, no mere formality. Throughout the year in question the public jails, especially the Edinburgh Tolbooth,

---

[1] *History*, vol. vii. p. 337.

[2] 8th July 1689. 'The Lord High Com^r His Grace and Lords of his Matie^s Privy Council do heirby grant warrant to incarcerat the Laird of Lagg within the Tolbooth of Edinr. till furder order.'—*MS. Records of Privy Council.*

were crammed with prisoners, as the number of petitions for release, to be found in the Privy Council Records, show. The miseries to which the unfortunate inmates were exposed could perhaps be properly realised only by one who remembered the narrow, gloomy interior of the old Edinburgh Tolbooth. It gave the idea—as he writes—of the crowd of prisoners packed in it ' much like the inmates of an emigrant ship.' [1]

Only three months before the date of these occurrences the new Government, under the presidency of the Duke of Hamilton, had adopted their ' Declaration of Estates and Claim of Right,' by which it was sought to render it illegal to imprison persons without expressing the reasons of their confinement. It was also demanded that delay in bringing suspects to trial, and torture without evidence, should be declared contrary to law. Still, under King William, prisoners seemed to be confined simply to get them out of the way. Torture *with* evidence was by no means dispensed with, though it had long been abolished in England.

Accordingly, by the end of August, Sir Robert and others of his fellow-prisoners forwarded petitions for liberation, in which they represented that

[1] Dr. Robert Chambers, *Domestic Annals*, vol. iii. p. 11.

they had been incarcerated since the 8th July, although they were unconscious of anything which
could deprive them of the liberty of subjects. It
was also complained that, among other miseries,
they were 'obnoxious to a most malignant fever'
then raging in the prison.

The following entry in the Minutes of the
Privy Council is connected with this incident:—
'Anent a Petitione given in to the Lords of their
Matie' privy Council by Sir Robert Greirsone of
Lagg; Shewing that wheras the petitioner was
upon the Eight day of July last impryssioned
within the Tolbooth of Edin. by the saids Lords
order, and, seeing his health is much indangered
. . and that there was a malignant fever broke
out in the prison q'of on is allready dead and
another very sick, and that he was content to
find suficient cautione to appear . . and therefore
humbly suplicating to the effect aforementioned.
The Lords . . ordaine the petitioner to be sett at
Libertie, granting bond and finding Cautione to
live peaceably . . under King William and Queen
Mary ; and that he shall not act, counsel, or con-
trive anything to their prejudice, nor converse or
correspond with rebbells etc. . . . and that he shall
appear when called under the penalties of Ane

Thousand ffive hundred pounds Sterling.'—Dated 23d Augt., 1689.[1]

John Lothian, who petitioned on 19th August, was likewise liberated. While they lay in prison the affair of Killiecrankie had come and passed; and there was the less risk in setting these men free.

The next two years were a period of the greatest unrest. The Whig Government was anything but secure. In June 1690 there was a threat of invasion by the French, which had the effect of exciting the sympathy of all classes on the side of order, and of bringing down increased severity on the Jacobites. Still, in the following year the brave, cunning, and unscrupulous Marlborough was so convinced that James held the winning hand that he risked his fortunes and reputation in a scandalous plot which the Jacobites themselves disclosed. What part, if any, Lag took in these plots is not known, but he seems to have shared in the severities that ensued.

How long Sir Robert enjoyed his liberty after his second imprisonment in the Edinburgh Tolbooth is uncertain. Early in the year 1692, however, we find him again a captive, this time in the

[1] MS. Records in Register House, Edinburgh.

Canongate Tolbooth, suffering under many grievous ailments, which a protracted confinement in
the filthy prison had aggravated, if it had not
caused.

Many of his companions were undergoing their
second, some their third year of captivity in these
abodes of wretchedness, to the great detriment of
health.

Whether or not he was set at large at once on
a representation of his present misery does not
appear.   But there has been preserved a State
paper purporting to be a 'List of Persons of
greatest note under bond to appear before the
Privy Council when called for.' [1]

On this list, the date of which is probably some

---

[1] Original in Hist. Depart. Register House.   There is on
this list of malcontents, besides the Laird's, the names of
several of the principal noblemen and many of the gentlemen
of the south of Scotland who favoured the Stuart cause, all,
with their cautioners, bound under heavy penalties according
to their means—most of them marked 'call.'   Amongst those
mentioned are the Earl of Arran, principal, Lords Morton and
Panmuir cautioners, £3,500; Earl of Hume with Lord
Southeske, 30,000 merks; cautioners for the Earl of Perth
(Drummonds and Hays), £5000; Maxwell of Springkell,
6,000 merks; Maxwell of Barnbochley, £100; Capt. John
Johnstone, with Westerhall as cautioner, 500 merks; Scots-
tarvet, 20,000 merks, etc.

time in the early part of 1693, the names of Sir
Robert Grierson as principal, and James Grierson
of Capenoch as cautioner, appear with the ominous
word 'call' added in the margin, showing that he
had been released, but that his subsequent conduct
had not been satisfactory, or that he had failed to
pay the heavy fines imposed on him.

What are apparently the reasons for this 'call,'
and the causes of his next incarceration, which
shortly ensued, are clearly set forth in a new bond
which Sir Robert and his kinsman and cautioner
Capenoch were constrained to enter into for Lag's
submission to the Government and liberation from
confinement.   In this document it is narrated how
Sir Robert had been imprisoned in the Canongate
Tolbooth for failing to make payment of a year's
valued rent of his estate, in which he had been
fined by the Lords in Council, on the 23d January
1693, 'for refusing the oath of allegiance and
assurance.'   This was a period of increased rigour
against the Jacobites.

Lag seems to have grown weary of this severe
treatment, which, with his failing health, overcame
for the time his obstinate resistance to the Government.   Accordingly orders were given by the
Lords of the Council on the 9th of November, for

his enlargement, Lag and his cautioner agreeing
now to make good the fine, and ' pay to Sir Thomas
Moncrieff of that Ilk, General Receiver of their
Majesties crown rents, the said year's valued rent.' [1]

Eight years after the Revolution had been
accomplished, great part of which had been passed
in durance, we once more find this incorrigible
offender against Whig rule, and inveterate ' non-
compounder,' appearing with his standing cautioner
Capenoch to give surety for his good conduct on
liberation.   Orders had been given to the Magistrates of Edinburgh and keeper of the prison
—both alike, by this time, tired of the Laird's
company—as Lag himself words it, ' to sett me at
liberty furth thereof,' on giving sufficient security
for the future, this time under penalty of one
thousand pounds sterling. [2]

When the new *régime* appeared to be fairly
established, it was but natural that thoughts of
redress, if not of revenge, should occur to the
sufferers in the recent troubles, or their relatives.
The Commission appointed to inquire into the
truth of what a ' Gentleman in Scotland' had
alleged in a ' Letter to a Friend in London ' re-

[1] MS. bond in Register House.   [2] *Ibid.*

garding the doings in the West Highlands, having carried out their instructions in 1695, the idea seems to have suggested itself to some persons that a similar inquiry would be only appropriate in the case of Sir Robert Grierson and his doings. The draft of a petition exists, in which the writer prays that as the ' Estates of Parliament have been at a great deall of pains in vindicating the honoure and justice of the nation in the mater of Glencoe,' so the Estates may ' give commission to such persons as they shall think fit for apprehending and receiving the person of the abovementioned Lagg, till judgment may be execute upon him.'

This paper is headed ' Memorandum anent a petition to be presented to the Parliament against Sir Robert Grierson of Lagge ; ' it is not signed by the petitioner, and it is not known if it ever was presented. In it special reference is made to the case of ' Marget Lauchlison ' and ' Marget Wilson ;' and to that of Mr. Bell of Whiteside and his companions in misfortune.

But there was still further degradation in store for the Laird. A charge of a very disgraceful sort was brought against him, which could not fail to vex and exasperate the old Tory gentleman, who

by this time had reason to know what persecution meant. Being a man under suspicion, and
dangerous to the Government, a ready ear was
no doubt given to anything likely to tell to his
discredit.

He was, in effect, charged with clipping and un-
lawful washing or 'minishing' of the good current
coin; and coining false money. In the precise
language of the indictment preferred against him
by Sir James Steuart of Goodtrees, Lord Advocate,
in June 1696, the offence is thus described:—

That he, Sir Robert Greir or Grierson, 'shaking
off all fear of God, respect to his Majesty's laws
and regaird to his own qualitie and honour, has
presumed to comit the said crime.' Namely, that
in the months of May to October last he 'sett' or
let the house called the Castle of Rockhill, a remote place suitable for such work, and 'got good
broad and millned money, and caused the same to
be clipped, and of the clippings of the good broad
money itself did cause false money or false Ducat-
downs, Dollars and other pieces which were for the
greatest pairt adulterat to be coyned ; and did vent
the same.'

Also, it was charged, that he furnished certain
materials and instruments as 'brass plates or pans,'

'Cisars,' a quantity of 'Allobast' and 'Tark, or Talcum,' the allobast being brought from Edinburgh, and the talcum from London, which are ingredients known to be used in false coining. Likewise it was charged that Sir Robert 'took pains for to observe what could be learnt at his Majesty's Mint in Edinburgh,' and that three books were found at Rockhill containing directions for mixing metals and whitening them.

For all this, if proved, it was held he ought to be punished with the forfeiture of life, lands, and goods.

Conceive what a crime to charge upon an honourable Scottish gentleman! We are not told what torrents of wrath the accusation called forth from a nature not the most gentle or submissive. We can fancy them.

To try this highly melodramatic case there was assembled on the 22d of June (the case having been 'continued' for a week) the full bench of justiciary judges, and a formidable array of counsel on both sides.[1]

---

[1] *MS. Books of Adjournal.* There were present the Earl of Lothian, Lord Justice-General; Adam Cockburn of Ormiston; [Sir] Colin Campbell of Aberuchill; David Home of Crossrig; [Sir] John Lauder of Fountainhall; Arch. Hope of Rankeillor;

There were lengthened informations for and against the prisoner, and many ingenious arguments as to whether 'clipping,' in as much as it did not make an impure or false coin, but only one that the receiver might see for himself was a little smaller than usual, was a crime demanding the death of the person convicted of it, and suchlike talk.   But when all was done, and the case fully stated, it seemed so absurd that the Advocate did not even call a witness—not an instrument and not a coin was produced—and he proceeded to crave that the 'dyet' might be deserted.

The explanation of the affair was simply this. Sir Robert had let the house to certain persons interested in bringing to maturity a new scheme for stamping linen with ornamental patterns; apparently something of the nature of calico printing was aimed at.   The implements, etc., which had caused the ferment and suspicion in the neighbourhood, it appeared, belonged to one Shochon, who stayed with Fraser, the tenant of Rockhall.   The former 'was a seal-cutter,

and James Falconar of Phesdo, judges.   The pursuers were the Lord Advocate and Sir Patrick Hume, his Majesty's Solicitor ; for the defence, Hew Dalrymple (afterwards Lord President) ; David Cunnynghame ; David Forbes ; and Archibald Sinclair.

practised engraving, and had a trade in stamping
linning : he engraved or carved the stamps himself.'
Sir Robert, it was shown, had not lived at Rockhall
for many years, and the house was not in a remote
place—on the contrary, there were fifteen families
resident in the near neighbourhood, and many in-
habited houses.

John Shochon was in Edinburgh in 1700, and
addressed a petition to Parliament regarding a new
method of manufacturing arras that he had in-
vented, ' the ground whereof is linen, and the
pictures thereof woolen, and all sorts of curious
colours, figures, and pictures.'[1]   From this we may
infer the exact nature of the mysterious doings at
Rockhall which brought such vexation to old Lag.

As time wore on we can understand how cases
that had been begun in the Civil Courts, and had
been interrupted by the troubles, were now revived.
The Laird of Lag figures in one of these ; he does
now no longer carry things with the high hand.

The case was one of a decree declaring an appeal
to Parliament by Lag in an action against him by
the Earl of Annandale to have fallen by default.
The Earl seems to have succeeded in obtain-

[1] *Acts of Scots Parliament,* quoted by Chambers.

ing, after much litigious debate, 'a decreet reduc-
tive,' as it is technically described, 'against the
Laird of Lag, reducing a bond alleged to have
been granted by the Earl of Hartfell, the pursuer's
father, to Grierson of Lagg.' The case at this
stage is not interesting, except for an incident in
the proceedings characteristic of the times. The
Earl of Annandale was amply supported in court
by friends and neighbours; Grierson was not present, nor any one to speak for him. It seems to
have been by chance that on this occasion a relative
of his was in Court, namely Sir David Thoirs,
whose wife was Lady Margaret,[1] sister of Lady
Henrietta Grierson. It was alleged that Lag was

---

[1] This lady had been previously married to Sir Alexander
Jardine, first baronet of Applegarth.

Charles Kirkpatrick Sharpe gives the following quaint description of her:—'The Duke's sister, Lady Margaret Jardine,
carried love of money to a pitch scarcely credible. Though
married to an opulent baronet, she would, for a halfpenny,
bear people on her shoulders across the river Annan, which
flows near the wall of her spouse's mansion; and, when there
was a fair or a field-preaching in the neighbourhood, would sit
on the banks of the stream the whole day in expectation of
customers. She generally wore rags; but, when visiting, carried
articles of finery in a napkin, which she would slip on before
she entered the house.'—Hoddam MS., *Mem. of Dundee*, i.
252.

out of the country, and delay craved; but it was
forcibly represented by the other side that—'it
was very easie for persons who live upon the
English borders to slip over the border when they
hear they are to be cited at a partie's instance, and
so frustrate the law.'   It was of no avail that the
Lady Henrietta Grierson had testified that at the
time of summons her husband was not at home.[1]

The origin of this case appears to have been a
suit instituted by Sir Robert Grierson against the
Earl of Annandale, in the year 1697, a report of
which is to be found in the law books.

At that date Sir Robert, it seems, charged
the Earl of Annandale for payment of £10,000,
contained in his grandfather's bond of 1654, with
the 'annual rents' accruing since.   To this answer
was made that Annandale's grandfather, the Earl
of Hartfell, gave to Lag of that day a disposition
of his 'hail moveable estate.'   Lag delivered to the
Earl factory blank in the factor's name.   The Earl
was empowered to fill up the name of anybody
he pleased in the blank, and 'to intromit with the
moveables,' which, it was alleged, showed that the
bond had been originally a trust, contrived to
'palliate the Earl's moveables from poinding,' the

[1] *Acts of Scottish Parliament*, 1700, vol. x. p. 225.

owner being then, 'in Oliver's time,' in bad circumstances with the Government and under great debts, considering especially that none would have lent him £10,000 on his single bond. Further, the matter had been latent forty years; and when Lag had claimed other sums he never had mentioned this.

Some of the Lords were not satisfied with these arguments, in view of the long minority in the Lag family, and the fact of the bond having been ' amissing.' In the end the majority thought it ' *merely a trust* and a convenience to save the Earl's moveables.'

Lag entered a protestation for ' remeid of law ' against this decree ; [1] with the ultimate result which has been stated.

This is about the last we hear of Sir Robert Grierson in his public life. What remains to be told relates rather to family history. And at this stage it may be asked, Was Lag a man in whom 'the invasive activities of evil' were preternaturally strong? It is a hard theory that a man can never do anything at variance with his

[1] Fountainhall, i. 768; *Dic. of Decisions*, 18th Feb. 1697, M. 16185.

own nature; and that he carries within him the germ of every action.

Claverhouse chafed and fretted under a sense of the ignoble work, beneath the dignity of a soldier, he was called on to perform. Whether Lag had any such feeling, or if his thought was no higher than the instinct of the police officer, acting under orders, we cannot know with certainty. But the particulars of his life now submitted may afford material for an approximate estimate of his character if not for a definite answer to the questions.

What has been here related of him has been taken, for the most part, from sources perhaps not absolutely free from exaggeration. But these accounts hardly show Lag to have been a man whose nature had fallen to the point of brutality reached by some of the leaders of his party—Rothes, for instance, disclaiming apologetically that he was *not* 'wearie of causing hang those damn'd fulls;'[1] or General Dalyell with his cold ferocity and glib talk of 'extirpation,' confident, as he wrote, that it was 'not posible to do vithout the inhabetens [of the South Country] be remouet or destroiet."[2]

[1] *Lauderdale Papers*, ed. by Osmund Airy (Camden Soc.), vol. ii. 1885.
[2] *Ibid.* vol. i. p. 255.

In Sir Robert Grierson we have the figure of a
Tory gentleman of the old Malignant type, of a
stamp more common at a period prior to his own
time; keen for the exercise of authority, whether
the king's or his own;[1] who could not be wrong
so long as he had the royal sanction, seeing his
'Sovereign Lord the King was immediate under
God within his own dominions,' according to a
formula of an earlier period of the Stuart rule.
With the idea of rebellion to be put down, little
thought had he for the enforcement of unjust law
upon a people of stubborn strength of will and
power of imagination, who believed themselves
to be 'in secure alliance with the unseen but
Supreme Power.'

Possibly, 'it was in him to go straight if the
times had been quieter,' and it may have been his
misfortune that his lines were cast where and when
they were. A spotted but *not* inconstant man;

---

[1] After the date of the Revolution Sir Robert Grierson still
exercised his authority as a Baron of Regality and of the Barony
of Lag in which he had been confirmed by Charles II. (*Acts of
Scottish Parliament*). At Burnside Hill, near Lag, at the period
in question, it is said he tried, condemned, and hanged a sheep-
stealer. This is believed to have been the last instance in
Nithsdale of a criminal suffering death by the sentence of a
Baron Bailie.—Grose's *Scottish Antiquities*, vol. i. p. 154.

a man of staunch fidelity to his king; with such qualities as were his he might, under other circumstances, have served his country well, and with more credit to himself.

Unhappily the one chance there was of retrieving his reputation he was not permitted to avail himself of. Had it been possible for him to have joined his illustrious colleague in the splendid effort of self-devotion in behalf of his sovereign, which has had the effect of rendering the Claverhouse who hunted poor wretches over the muirs of Galloway unrecognisable in the noble Dundee, striking one last blow in the cause of his exiled king—his memory would have been differently regarded.

BETWEEN THE REBELLIONS.

IT was not exactly a text of Scripture to which these old Jacobites were wont to refer, in tossing off a sympathetic glass ; but rather an artful simulation of religion with well-bridled tongue, when they mentioned significantly—' JAMES III. and viii.'

CHAPTER VI.

As the districts of the South-West were those on which the rod of persecution had fallen most heavily, so when the time of trial—in which true religion had shone forth in simple purity—was overpast, the reaction was strikingly apparent. The triumph of Presbytery was complete ; but ten years had not passed by before it was seen that the blood of the Martyrs had purchased a state of security and ease, with all the concomitant evils, of which those responsible for the well-being of the Church could not fail to be ashamed.

A very remarkable manuscript document exists, and is now before me, in which a striking picture is presented of the condition of the clergy and people in several of the parishes of this district. It consists of a record of the proceedings of a Committee appointed by the Synod of Galloway in

1697, to inquire into the truth of certain rumours that had reached them, regarding the state of scandalous neglect prevailing. It is highly important historically, and of interest as bearing on the subject of this sketch; but as it is somewhat lengthy, it has been deemed expedient to give a short abstract of the document in the Appendix.[1] So far as I am aware, it has not been printed hitherto.

Though there was the falling away in religious life shown in these reports, there was little in the bitterness of feeling towards those who had taken an active part in the repression of the Whigs. It is very evident indeed what would have been the style of rule in Scotland had the leaders of the now triumphant Church been permitted to have the full sway they desired, and unchecked authority to turn the tables upon their adversaries. The disappointment of Principal Carstares,[2] and others, was very sincere when they found there was a power in the State higher than themselves that meant to take cognisance of Church affairs. King William had fallen upon a skilful device to get rid of the most turbulent spirits of the South-West, by enrolling

[1] See Appendix No. 1.
[2] Conf. *Life and Times of William Carstares*, D.D.

the Cameronians in a regiment by themselves. It
is on record how this splendid body of soldiers
fought, prayed, and protested in their own way,
guided by their own chaplain, Alexander Shields;
but Patrick Walker, the pedlar, recounts[1] how
they too fell away, and that 'salvation' was *not* the
word most familiar in their mouths, for it was in
Flanders that they served—in Uncle Toby's time.

This tendency to depart from the strict discipline of the Covenanting age, and an inclination
towards Episcopacy, more than once remarked
upon with apprehension by Wodrow in his private
note-books,[2] were among the causes that led the
General Assembly to call for the parish records
of sufferings that have been mentioned. This
collection was made, as has been shown, between
the years 1708, when first the idea was started, and
1711. It was not till ten years later that Wodrow's
great work of compilation was completed.

Those appear to have somewhat to go upon
who affirm that while the records of this period
have been placed

'Under the blanching vertical eye-glare'

of recent criticism, no one has fared better than

---

[1] See *Biographia Presbyteriana.*   [2] See *Analecta,* passim.

Robert Wodrow. It was the custom to follow Sir Walter Scott, and style him the 'mendacious' historian of the Church, and to use even stronger terms. But it has been seen, at all events in one notable case, with what care the parish reports which he adopted were prepared; and it is not improbable that other narratives were equally well considered, and that some touches of picturesque embellishment only are his own.

The case is different with Patrick Walker, the pedlar,[1] the fanatical, vain-glorious, and illiterate collector of Covenanting tales. Such a man had, of course, some words to say regarding Sir Robert Grierson, and very unpleasant words they are. The source being such, they need not be further noticed. There seems reason to believe that the researches made at this time into bygones were a means of fanning into life many of the embers

---

[1] Patrick Walker is believed to have been the prototype of David Deans in *The Heart of Mid-Lothian*. There his fanatical absurdities are amusing and picturesque, which can hardly be said of his own writings. His value as an authority may be estimated by the following note annexed to one of his biographies :—

'P.S. If any person has any Passages in the Lives of thir Worthies . . . let them send them to my House at Bristo Port and they *shall be printed.'—Biog. Presbyteriana.*

which a period of rest had permitted in some degree to cool.

At this time Sir Robert took up his abode at Rockhall, which, as has been stated, came to the Lag family as *tocher* with Isobel Kirkpatrick of Closeburn, when she married Roger Grierson in 1468. The old mansion of Rockhall, which is not of this venerable age, stands on a slight elevation commanding an extensive view of the Solway Firth and the Cumberland hills, not far from the village of Collin, some three miles south of Dumfries, on the English road.[1]

At the time Rockhall was occupied by Lag, it was a long three-storied building, the lower story divided in three parts strongly arched. One of them is now used as a kitchen, another as a wine cellar ; in the centre of the arch of the latter is an iron hook twelve inches long of inch-round iron, from which 'old Lag' is said to have suspended Covenanters by the neck.

There was also attached to the house a small

---

[1] A seisin of Rockhall to Nicholas Maxwell, spouse of Sir William Grierson of Lag, Kt., dated 1st May 1610, mentions— ' All and haill the place of Rockhall laitlie biggit be the said Sir William,' etc.—*Reg. of Seisins*, Dumfries.

turret or look-out tower, traces of which still remain.

The events which have been described left Sir Robert Grierson broken in health, and seriously embarrassed in fortune. Besides, by the heavy fines imposed on him, there is reason to believe his estate was much impoverished by the demands of the Duke of Queensberry, with whose sister he had the honour to be allied, as, in the preceding generation, the Grierson family had suffered for their attachment to James, second Earl of Queensberry, the duke's father. In the family 'tree' reference is made to an arrangement, not very clearly stated, 'for relief of cautionry and debts,' in which Robert Grierson of Lag, who died in 1666, and Sir Robert, our hero, who succeeded him, were bound for James, Earl of Queensberry. It is well known that the first Duke of Queensberry spent fabulous sums in making Drumlanrig Castle the magnificent building it is. The accounts connected with the work were so appalling that the owner sealed them up, and wrote this malediction on the cover: 'Deil pike out his een that looks on thir.' The doings of Queensberry, the *Deil's Duke*, as he has been styled in tradition, who spent only one night in this palace, are credited by the Grierson family with much of the pecuniary embarrassment that afterwards overtook them.

In the year 1708 the hopes of the Jacobites were high. The French were on the sea. Their desires, they thought, were at the very point of fruition. But expectation was not destined to be fulfilled. The second Duke of Queensberry was suspected of intriguing; [1] several Scottish gentlemen were brought to trial for their too open sympathy with the projected invasion, and through rare good luck were acquitted. How Lag—burning with all the fervour of the confident heart—bore himself at this time we have little direct evidence to show.

When, however, the first great 'opportunity,' as the Jacobites phrased it, occurred in 1715, Sir Robert Grierson did not himself join in the enterprise; but he sent forward his eldest son, William, then a youth, and Gilbert, his fourth son, who must have been but a boy, to join, along with many of the Border gentlemen, both Catholics and Protestants, Lord Kenmure's rash expedition into England in the cause of hereditary right. [2]

---

[1] *Secret History of Colonel Hooke's Negociations in Scotland in favour of the Pretender*, 1760.

[2] There were some, however, who were prepared to dispute

Their discomfiture at Preston is a melancholy incident. Of the 1460 rebels who fell into the enemy's hands about one thousand were Scotch. Amongst these were Nithsdale; Kenmure; Basil Hamilton of Baldoon, lieutenant of Kenmure's troop of horse; William Grierson, younger of Lag, and his brother Gilbert. Also Riddel of Glenriddel; Edmund Maxwell of Carnsalloch; William Maxwell of Munches, and George his brother; Maxwell of Cowhill; and many more.[1] All these —indeed all the captives of rank and distinction —were ordered to be conveyed to London, which they reached on the 9th of December, in miserable plight; their arms pinioned with cords—the

even the right of birth to the Chevalier St. George. This is how they wrote :—' He [JAMES the King] had no Son to inherit the Land, but, yielding to the devices of JEZEBEL, his Queen, he consented to all she did and own'd a spurious issue to be his Legitimate Heir; and called his name JAMES.'—*Proper Lessons for the Tories to be used throughout the year :* London, 1716.

[1] See *Hist. of the late Rebellion raised against* KING GEORGE *by the Friends of the Popish Pretender :* by Peter Rae, Dumfries, 1718, p. 325.

' A list of the Noblemen, Gentlemen, Followers, or Servants of those who surrendered prisoners at Preston,' is given in a work entitled *A Faithful Register of the Late Rebellion :* London, 1718. The names of William Grierson (with his attendants James Dalgleish, Geo. Carrick, and Cha. Donaldson) and Gilbert Grierson appear upon it.

customary treatment of criminals;—each man's horse led by a private soldier. They were thus taken through the streets of the metropolis, the objects of every species of insult and scurrilous abuse.

How the Earl of Derwentwater and Viscount Kenmure [1] suffered on Tower Hill is well known ; as is also the story of the escape of Lord Nithsdale from his prison, through the devotion of his heroic wife. Fines, forfeiture of estate, and attainder were the punishment of the rest. There is a family tradition that William Grierson was tried and sentenced to death, and that for six weeks he lay in the Tower, his coffin in one corner of his cell, waiting the time when the headsman should call him out and deal with him. But this is certainly an exaggeration. There is, however, no doubt that a heavy fine was laid on the lands of Lag on account of his treason. The sum appears

---

[1] William Gordon, sixth Viscount Kenmure, son of Alexander, fifth Viscount, and Marion M'Culloch of Ardwell, already mentioned, succeeded his father in 1698; and raised the Stuart standard at Lochmaben 12th October 1715. 'A grave full-aged gentleman of singular good temper, with no experience in military affairs.' He was tried and condemned for Treason, January 1716, and beheaded 24th February of the same year.

to have been a year's rent of the estate as determined by a strict valuation.[1]

Though the fine levied upon William Grierson was a heavy one, it is very certain that in the long-run he and his father fared better than they had any reason to expect. The circumstances of their case and Lag's measures in defence of his estate in opposition to the officers of the Crown are, though somewhat complicated, very curious.

After the Rebellion of 1715, and the wholesale forfeiture of lands of those who had engaged in it, a body of officials was called into existence, by an Act of Parliament,[2] entitled the Commissioners of Forfeited Estates, whose duty it was to ad-

[1] 'Abstract of the several Forfeited Estates Real lying in Scotland, taken by the Surveyor and his Deputy upon the oaths of the several Tenants, Possessors, etc., by order of the Commissioners of Enquiry in the years 1716 and 1717, containing the particular Rent and the yearly value thereof:'—

Rental of the Real Estate of William Greir, Junior of Lagg.
Money. Rent payable in Money, . . . £424, 15s. od.

Among the Estates forfeited appear, Nithsdale, £808, 2s. 3d.; Kenmure, £643, 3s. 11d; Wintoun, £3393, 10s; Mar, £1884, 9s. 2d; and Carnwath, £864, 8s. 2d.—Charles' *Trans. in Scotland*: Stirling, 1816, ii. 447.

[2] 'An Act for appointing Commissioners of the Estates of certain Traitors, and of Popish Recusants, and of Estates given to superstitious uses; in order to raise money out of them severally for the use of the Publick.'—1 Geo. I., c. 20.

minister the large possessions of the convicted rebels, or to sell them if necessary, for the public good. They were, for the most part, men of great Parliamentary experience. Sir Richard Steele was one of them. Their instructions were, however, framed entirely on an English model, with no reference to Scots law or custom. They 'dealt summarily with the estates as if they were so much contraband goods in the hands of revenue officers.'[1]

Naturally these gentlemen very shortly came into collision with the Scots law authorities; and the Commissioners complained in their representations to the Government that they were interrupted in transacting their business by a body calling itself the Court of Session, which exercised so much authority in Scotland, that the Commissioners could find no means of getting their orders put in force.

The Scots judges defended their position, and the laws of the country as guaranteed by the Treaty of Union, pointing out that they had not been consulted prior to the passing of the Act, with which they had become acquainted accidentally.

Though ultimately the Commissioners prevailed, an appeal was provided from their decisions to a

[1] Hill Burton's *Hist.* vol. viii. p. 349.

Court of Delegates consisting of the judges of the Court of Session.

On the attainder of William Grierson, a sentence of forfeiture seems to have been passed upon the Grierson estates. So early as the 26th October 1713 Sir Robert had by a deed of entail named his son William his heir, whom failing, his other children in succession. He had done more. He had actually placed William in possession of the estates by infeftment; and his eldest son thus became 'fear of Lag,' his father retaining the life-rent. This was done, it is hinted, in view of Sir Robert's old age and infirmity.

But the transfer of the estates was not uncon-ditional. The deed of 1713 contains the remark-able 'irritant clause' or stipulation, that in case Sir Robert should be in danger of arrest for debt, then it should be imperative that William Grierson (or the heir in possession at the time) should relieve Sir Robert 'within the space of six months after personal intimation to him ' (the heir); or, in case he should not be found readily, the intimation should be held to be sufficient, if made at the mansion place of Rockhall, Lag, or Laghall. Any failure in this proviso rendered the deed of no effect.[1]

[1] *Register of Tailzies*, Hist. Dept., Register House.

Moreover, Lag provided that while he himself might sell as much of the estate as might be necessary to pay his debts, none of his successors should be at liberty to do so. Also he declared that any deed done, any crime committed, 'or even (as God forbid) the cryme of Treasone'— this phrase occurs with ominous reiteration— should affect the doer only, not the estate.

This deed had not been long in existence when disagreement arose between Lag and his son. Sir Robert wished to sell, as provided for, some portions of his estates to satisfy his creditors. There were persons in Dumfries ready enough to buy the lands in question,[1] as they were desirable possessions; but they declined to complete any bargain without the concurrence of William, the heir. He, on his part, as a deponent stated in the course of the law proceedings that ensued, 'refused to agree unless Sir Robert gave him all, or a part of the price.' But Sir Robert declared that 'he designed to apply the same for the payment of his debts for which *he lay under distress.*'

Upon which, says another witness, Sir Robert Grierson 'took four instruments against his son

[1] Namely 'Betwixt the Waters;' 'Nethertown;' 'Boigs;' 'Priestlands,' etc.

I

William, between 7th April 1714 and January 1715.' These steps, it is perhaps proper to add, were merely legal measures.

Thus it will be seen that when the short-lived Rebellion of '15 had run its course, and William had been convicted for his share in it, and his property forfeited by his treason, Lag was in a position to resist the Commissioners of Estates, with the plea that, although his eldest son had been infeft in the lands, yet the provisions of the deed which effected this had been infringed in such a manner as to annul it. In effect Lag had been under distress for debt without the required relief; and the estates were consequently his.

It was not to be expected that the Commissioners would see the matter in this light. Therefore in August 1719, at Lag's instance, the case of ' Sir Robert Grierson, Bart. of Lag, in exception ' against the Commissioners and Trustees of the Publick,' was submitted to Lord Pollock, a judge in the Court of Session, in the first instance, in accordance with the terms of the Act already mentioned.

It was as little to be expected that, seeing the

' *Exceptio* was the Roman law-term for a defence to an action, and was adopted by early Scotch lawyers. *Conf.* Indices to Stair's *Institutions*, and Erskine's *Institute.*

jealousy that existed between the Commissioners and the Court of Session, and the general feeling of opposition towards them throughout the country, that any point of law of nicety or doubt that might arise in discussion would be seen as they presented it. Accordingly, when the terms of Lag's entail of 1713, with its peculiar conditions, was examined, and the Commissioners represented to the Judges that this was merely a scheme by means of which he hoped his personal debts might be settled for him, and that they were prepared to stand in place of the heir, and do all that he could have done, my Lords were of another opinion, and held that the ' irritant clause ' in the entail could not be got over.[1]

[1] The following is the report of this curious case as it appears in the law-books, with all the technicalities :—' Grierson of Lagg against his eldest son and the officers of State ; between 1716 and '25.'—' One having contracted some personal debt, tailzied his estate with this irritant clause—" That in case the tailzier should happen to be charged with horning, or other diligence done against him, that the heirs of tailzie must relieve him thereof within six months after intimation thereof, otherwise to amit and lose their right." The irritancy being incurred, the public, by a forfeiture coming in the place of the heirs of tailzie, it was *argued* that the design of this clause was nothing else but to relieve the tailzier of his present debt ; and here the public was ready to purge the irritancy and answer to the tailzier for all damage sustained. The Lords found the irritancy not purgeable.'—MAXWELL MORISON's *Dic. of Decisions*, 7272.

Perhaps it was to make matters still more secure that Sir Robert the very next day after this decision in his favour—namely, on the 28th of August 1719—executed another deed of entail, in which William was not mentioned.

So matters rested for a little while.

Though Sir Robert had withdrawn himself from public life even before the rising of 1715, there is evidence that he still took interest in all political questions, and, as might be expected, could on occasion express a stout Jacobite opinion in language possessing much of his wonted vigour. In 1718 the Rev. Peter Rae put out, at Dumfries, his *History of the late Rebellion*, from which some quotations have already been made. In the opening chapter he discusses the scheme said to have been laid down by the Tory Ministry and Parliament during the last four years of Queen Anne to cut off the Protestant succession and settle the crown on the 'Popish Pretender,' which the author takes to have been the foundation of the recent rebellion. In the same chapter, in detailing the state of affairs in Scotland at that period, he writes : 'In the beginning of her Reign the Scots Episcopal Clergie, having conceived great hopes from the promises of her Ministry, used their utmost endeavours with the Scottish Parliament to obtain a Toleration. But this was strongly opposed by the Established Church of that kingdom, who knew them to be enemies to the Revolution, and at length was refused even by the then Tory Parliament.' (Chap. i. p. 3.)

In the copy of Rae's *History* which belonged to the Rockhall family, there is written, in what is believed to be Lag's own handwriting, the following characteristic remark upon this passage—and it is remarkable as being one of the very few specimens remaining of Lag's writing :—

' This is a damn'd lie, for the E. of Strath[more] presented the Act and the Episcop. clergy solicite against it ; and told that they wold not accep being that they would be oblig'd to qualifie soe that the Act was dropt by the E.'

William Grierson, younger of Lag, married in 1720 ' Mistress Anne Musgrave,' third daughter of Sir Richard Musgrave of Haytoun in Cumberland. There is a letter written by Winifred, Countess of Nithsdale, to her sister-in-law, Lady Traquair, dated 21st February 1721, in which she says, ' I am glad young Lag has got so good a fortune.'[1] So it seems the match was considered to be a good one.   In consequence of this event, the settlement of his estates that Sir Robert had made was upset.

By this time William had again been received into his father's good graces; and another deed of entail, dated 22d October 1725, was executed by Lag, in which due provision was made for the young wife, the same conditions as to his debts being made as before.   At the same time Sir Robert specified that the very modest allowance of £166, 13s. 6d. yearly should be allotted to himself, and a further sum of £8 to provide him with a house.   In this deed mention is made of the pardon granted on the 29th June 1724 by the clemency of King George I., which enabled him to take and hold anything to which he might become entitled after that date.

Thus he was once more placed in possession of his father's estates by 'infeftment.'   The Laird must have been at this time—if the data regarding his age be correct—about eighty-eight years old.   From these details it may be seen how far it was Lag's intention to 'disinherit' his eldest son, as spoken of in one of the most recent books of the Baronetcy.

[1] *Book of Caerlaverock*, vol. ii. p. 223.

Regarding Lag's other children it may be briefly stated that James, his second son, about whom little is known, was at the Scots College at Douay from 1698 to 1700.[1] Shortly before his death he seems to have been put in possession by his father of certain lands in the parish of Troqueer. His wife was Elizabeth Fergusson. She survived her husband, who died early in 1722. Their son Robert, already mentioned, in some way incurred the displeasure of old Lag and of William his uncle. So much was this the case that, on the occasion of the death of Sir Robert, or of Lady Henrietta Grierson, it is on record that his uncle William refused to pay for a suit of mourning that had been ordered by the young Robert, of a tradesman in Dumfries. He was expressly cut off from succeeding to the family estates. This was done by a fourth deed which Lag executed a few days before his death, namely, on the 20th December 1733. In it Robert's name is removed from the series of heirs. It was of no avail that, on his uncle's death, he 'took out breaves' and had

[1] MSS. of Mrs. Dorothy Maxwell Witham of Kirkconnell and her husband, among which are two registers of the Scots College.—*Report of the Royal Com. of Hist. MSS.*, Rep. 6, pt. 1, 2.

himself served heir to the estates; but he could not be excluded from succession to the family title, and he became third Baronet in 1760, on William's death. So far as I am aware, no mention is made of him in the ordinary books of the Baronetcy.

His sister, Henrietta Grierson, married James Fergusson, surgeon in Dumfries.

Of Lag's third son, John, little more is known than that he died in 1730.[1] Some of the family details, now given for the first time, are established by an 'Inventory of Writs found in his trunk at his death,' on the 16th March.

Gilbert, who succeeded as fourth Baronet, has been mentioned, and will be further spoken of. He was a lawyer, and was Chamberlain to the Duke of Buccleuch, at Dalkeith.

Henrietta, Lag's only daughter, married Sir Walter Laurie of Maxwelton.

It was only in accordance with what we know of human nature that, as time ran on, many a grudge and bitter feeling remained in the hearts of those who had been out in the troubles, and

---

[1] The details of expenditure at his funeral are very curious. A few of the items are given as they appear in the original account, in Appendix No. 11.

of their children bred up with little idea of charity towards the persecutors. To a new generation the narratives became traditional, and received many an effective touch in the way of embellishment at the hands of imaginative relators. These had it in their power to deal out a certain measure of retribution, or to describe how retribution had already overtaken the chief actors in various ghastly forms of 'special providence.' The after careers of the persecutors were closely watched, and if punishment was not seen to fall upon them during active life, it was considered only justice that their latter end should be miserable. Thus it is a tradition how Irving, the fierce old Laird of Bonshaw, as he lay dying, in his rusty corselet, of the wound dealt him by one of his own followers, in the midst of his ravings of the flash of carbines before his eyes, and of the smell of gunpowder in his nostrils, at intervals—all too late—craved to make reparation for his misdeeds by dividing his inheritance among the children of those he had injured.

In their own districts especially such men fared badly. Tongues were exceptionally busy with Sir Robert Grierson in the districts of the South-West, where Lag continued to live in retirement

for full fifty years after the days of persecution.
As in the case of Laurie of Maxwelton, it was told
and believed of him, that, on one occasion when
he was handed a cup of wine, the contents turned
to blood in his hand.[1]

There used to be much curiosity to get a sight
of the *fell* old man. On one occasion, it is related,
an adventurous youth, to gratify his curiosity, asked
leave to carry in an armful of billets for the old
Laird's fire, as he sat in his great arm-chair by
the hearthside, at Rockhall. The old gentleman,
perhaps suspecting something, with a *look*, which
he never forgot, suddenly turned upon the attendant
and demanded—

'Ony Whigs in Gallawa' *noo*, lad ? '

The terror-stricken youth dropped his load of
wood upon the floor, and fled.

No better instance of the process by which folk-
tales are propagated could be adduced than in the

---

[1] This incident is referred to in *Old Mortality*. The manner
in which the fact is recorded in the case of Sir Robert Laurie
shows curiously how these 'special providences' were looked
for at this time—and consequently found. 'The Steward of
the said Maxwelton reported that a cup of wine delivered that
day, (after shooting of William Smith) into his hand turned into
congealed blood; be that as it will, *himself died from a fall
from his horse, some years after.'—Cloud of Witnesses.*

case of Sir Robert Grierson. His atrocities were the talk of the country-side, and were naturally compared with any similar barbarities that might come to be spoken of. Thus, when it happened that the old story of Regulus and the Carthaginians was referred to—how, when the conquered Roman Consul returned to Carthage according to his promise, having dissuaded his countrymen from making peace, the enraged Carthaginians put him into a barrel, the inside of which bristled with knives and spikes,—this ghastly incident, repeated in mediæval legends, would likely be cited as 'just the kind of thing old Lag would have done.' By degrees it would be said he *did* it. And now at the present day, both at Rockhall and Halliday Hill, near the old Tower of Lag, they point out the acclivities where 'Auld Lag,' not in the execution of any judicial process, but simply for his own amusement, used to roll down Covenanters in barrels into which had been fixed spikes and knives—exactly in the Carthaginian fashion.

In this instance there is no exception to the process so commonly seen in operation in the case of ancient myths that have become the property of the people. The incidents are complete in the first place, then allotted to the proper personage, and by degrees improved upon,[1] with that want of originality as regards imagination which led Dugald Stewart to use his famous simile of the barrel-organ, incapable of giving a single note beyond its one set of tunes.

There is much diversity of statement regarding the date of Lag's death. It is usually said in books bearing on the Covenanting age that he died on the 23d December 1733. It is so stated, for instance, in the *Cloud of Witnesses*, though the earlier editions of that work are of an age long before that period. This particular date appears on the title-page of a satirical poem directed against Sir Robert and the persecutors, to be mentioned hereafter, and this may be the authority for the date. The 15th April 1736 is given by Playfair in his *Scots' Baronetage*, and by other authors.

Some few years ago an interesting book—a battered little parchment volume—was discovered in the possession of one of the tenants on Rockhall estate, and has been forwarded to me through the kindness of Sir Alexander Grierson, the present Baronet of Lag. It is a tenant's receipt-book containing the signatures of old Lag and his son William, for annual rent of a farm during a

[1] Conf. *Custom and Myth*, by Andrew Lang, M.A., 1885.

succession of many years. As Sir Robert ceased to sign these receipts in the year 1727, and his son William continued to grant the discharges, it was too hastily assumed that the old Laird must have died between 1727 and 1728. But the arrangement already described, by which William was in possession of the estates during his father's lifetime, explains this.

As William Grierson, for some reason, was not served heir to his father till the 5th June 1740,[1] it was supposed that Lag had not then been long dead.

In the course of the researches for the purposes of this sketch, however, a law document[2] has very recently come to light, which leaves no doubt as to the date of the Laird's death. He died on the 31st day of December 1733.

Moreover the original manuscript accounts for the expenses incurred at his funeral are now before me. They confirm the statement now made as to the date of the old man's death.

There was a strange story, not yet forgotten, current in Nithsdale and Galloway.

[1] See *Index of Service of Heirs.*
[2] *Memorial with respect to the Settlement made by the Deceast Sir Robert Grierson of Lagg,* dated 4th February 1761.

One stormy night not far off Yule, a small
vessel was making her way up the Irish Sea, heavily
tacking against a northern blast, as she tried to
make the mouth of the Solway. The night was
very dark; but for momentary glimpses of the
moon as the gale sent the black clouds flying across
her face. During one of these the look-out man
descried, and reported, a strange sail on the larboard
quarter. At the next gleam of light a *very strange*
sail was on the beam, moving so as to cross their
bows. Every eye was strained peering into the
darkness. Between them and the horizon they
saw, as it were, a great State-coach, with a retinue
of footmen, torch-bearers, outriders, and coachman
complete, driving furiously. As the apparition
drew nearer, they all perceived how, with strange
clamour and unearthly crackings of his whip,
distinctly heard above the rattle of the cordage
and the roar of the storm, the coachman impelled
the ghostly equipage and its team of six horses
at headlong pace over the crests of the breaking
waves, and in the very teeth of the rising tempest.

It was not until the *cortége* was passing into the
distance that the skipper, with a conscience gener-
ated by a cargo of doubtful righteousness, recovered
presence of mind sufficient to enable him to hail, off

the forecastle—'Where from?' An answer came from out the darkness—'*From —— to Collyn.*' The port of departure was heard clearly enough. But no one in the ship dared to hint at the place they all knew had been named; which shows the state of terror that crew were in.

It is beyond the power of any ordinary pen adequately to describe the fearful incidents of this night as they linger in tradition. It was a high occasion for the warlocks, witches, and all evil beings in which the South of Scotland is so rich. And as darkness drew on, and the tempest rose on the Solway, there was held a perfect revelry of 'bogle-wark.'

> 'The hag is astride
> This night for to ride
> Though ne'er so foul be the weather;
> In a dirty hair lace
> She leads on a brace
> Of black boar-cats to attend her.'

Frightful personages and nameless things came trooping from every quarter, below and aloft; the trough of the sea was full of them. Headless horses, furiously galloping, issued from among the clouds. At noon of night the 'Spectre Dog of Man,' the dread 'Mauthe Hound,' came forth, whose bark bodes evil to passing ships; all these hasting to the spot where the Haunted Ships of the Solway—which only float on such occasions as this—had risen and, with every sail set, stood in all their former beauty, each one tenanted by an awesome crew. And through the black night was seen 'the streaming lights from their cabin windows, and were heard the sound of wild mirth and the clamour of tongues, and the unearthly whoop and halloo and song, ringing far and wide' across the sea.

'From these *Spectre Ships* there were shriekings cast
That were heard above the tempest blast!'

Nothing that Sir Walter Scott has ventured to set down regarding the old hero exceeds in horror the doings of that terrible night—when Lag was at his last end—and only he himself could have described them.

The popular accounts of Lag's last illness and burial are exceedingly grotesque. During the latter part of his life, Sir Robert had taken up his abode in his town lodging in Dumfries. It was an ancient pile of building, of singular construction, facing the principal part of the High Street of the town, known as the 'Plainstones.' This old house was called the 'Turnpike,' from the spiral staircase, a characteristic of it, as of many of the old Edinburgh houses; it was situated at the head of what was called the Turnpike Close, and little more than two hundred yards from the Nith. The best ◯ known of the many legends regarding Lag is this : that when he came near his end, and was sorely tormented with gout, he had relays of servants posted so as to hand up from one to another a succession of buckets of cold water from the Nith, that he might cool his burning limbs—but the moment his feet were inserted into the water, it began to *fizz* and *boil*.

In this old Turnpike house[1] Sir Robert died on the 31st December 1733. It is related that on this occasion a ' corbie'—*sib* perhaps to the hateful birds that Victor Hugo's sentry spoke

[1] M'Dowall's *History of Dumfries*, 2d ed., pp. 650-1. The following interesting scrap of traditionary information has been kindly communicated by the author of that excellent work :—
' An old antiquarian friend, long since dead, told me that Sir Robert had grown so corpulent in his latter days that his body could not be decently carried down the winding stair for burial; and that accordingly a portion of the wall between the two windows looking on to the Plainstones had to be temporarily removed, and that through the wide vacancy thus created the coffin was lowered down. My informant, who was old enough to remember all about the taking down of the lodging in 1826, added that the appearance of the wall between the windows justified the tradition.'

of ¹—of preternatural blackness and malignity of aspect, perched himself on the coffin, and would not be driven off, but accompanied the funeral *cortége* to the grave in the churchyard of Dunscore.

Moreover, when the funeral procession started, and had got some little way on the Galloway side of the Nith, it was found that the horses, with all their struggles, and dripping with perspiration, from some mysterious cause could move the hearse no further. Sir Thomas Kirkpatrick of Closeburn, the old friend and comrade of Lag (and his relative), who was believed to be deep in some branches of the Black Art,² was one of the mourners. This gentleman, the stoutest of Non-jurors, on this occasion swore a great oath that he would drive the hearse of Lag 'though —— were in it!' and ordered a team of beautiful Spanish horses of his own to be harnessed in place of the others. Sir Thomas mounted and took the reins, when the

---

¹ ' Un corbeau qui passait fit l'ombre dessus.
   "Les oiseaux noirs guidaient Judas cherchant Jésus ;
   Sire, vois ce corbeau," dit une sentinelle.'
                              La Confiance de Fabrice.

² A descendant of Sir Thomas Kirkpatrick informs me that the particular branch of occult science in which her ancestor was skilled, was called the ' Oxford Art '—whatever that may be.

horses instantly dashed off at a furious gallop that he could in no wise restrain, and abated nought of their headlong pace till they reached the church-yard of Dunscore, where they suddenly pulled up —and died.

At the present day these legends of Lag's latter end are still current. But there are facts not so well known.

There have been few occasions of rarer jollity than that of old Lag's funeral. With the last of the year '33 his chequered life went out; and straightway there set in a course of feasting and a flow of strong drink that apparently had begun before the poor man was dead, and ceased not during the first fortnight of the New Year; the monotony only occasionally broken by an agree-able change in the nature of the beverages.

There was much wine consumed before the burial. A goodly supply was sent out for con-sumption at the churchyard. On their return there was more systematic conviviality among the gentlemen, Lord Stormont, Sir Thomas Kirk-patrick, Maxwell of Carriel, and many others who, like Gilbert Grierson, had come from a distance to assist.

Some of the items of the account for funeral

expenses and all this festivity are appended;[1] they vary from the 'small clarit' at 1s. and 6d. a bottle to the 'stronger wine;' and the more elegant 'ffrantinack;' and brandy—haply from the Solway—at the reasonable price of eighteenpence a bottle. But special notice is asked to two charges —namely, the amount 5s. 6d. paid to 'Charles Herries, smith, for Iron work to the Hearse;' and 'to the Smith for Sir Thomas Kirkpatrick's horses 2sh.,' after the funeral.

There is a tradition, as I have been assured, by members of the Kirkpatrick family, that their ancestor certainly drove the hearse at Lag's funeral, and that the Spanish horses afterwards died as has been related. Is it not possible that there is in the two items quoted additional evidence that something *did* go wrong as the funeral procession wended its way from Dumfries to Dunscore? It is not difficult to see how a slight accident to the vehicle—a tire or a linch-pin defective, or a wheel jammed in a ridge of the road, on that winter day —may have necessitated a halt till the services of the smith could be obtained. Then some accident to Sir Thomas's horses, also calling for the attention of the smith, may have given rise to the

[1] See Appendix No. III.

stories, amplifying as they passed from mouth to mouth, regarding the events of that day,' on which something marvellous was looked for.

Thus the legends regarding our hero, which made his name a terror even after he was dead, were handed down and remained, until the pen which has given a picturesque aspect to so many incidents in Scottish history that they did not possess in themselves, drew a halo of romance around the name of Lag.

¹ Mr. John Kerr, factor for Sir Alexander Grierson, informs me that he has ' heard his grandfather say that his father followed Lag's funeral, led by the hand of his uncle William Hutchison, a tenant on the estate of Rockhall (the Hutcheon who figures in *Redgauntlet*), from the Turnpike Close to Maxwelltown on the other side of the river, and that nothing unusual happened so far.'

A PUNGENT PASQUIL.

——I did request mine honest friend Peter Proudfoot, travelling merchant, known to many in this land for his faithful and just dealings as well in muslin and cambrics as in small wares, to procure me, on his next peregrinations to that vicinage, a copy of the *Epitaphion*.

OLD MORTALITY.

CHAPTER VII.

A PUNGENT PASQUIL.

IT might be supposed that when Sir Robert was dead and gone there would also be an end of the evil spoken regarding him. This was, however, by no means the case. His memory was assailed with a species of weapon which has ever been in Scotland one of infinite keenness and point, by whatever name they have been called, whether 'libels,' 'cockalanes' or 'pasquils.' These usually venomous trifles are of high value for the light and local colour they are calculated to afford in every picture of the age to which they refer. Such things have scarcely yet met with the attention they deserve in this regard. One of these comes as a curious contribution to this sketch of Sir Robert Grierson's career. It is commonly known as ' *Lag's Elegy.*' Its full title is lengthy, and with much elaboration defines the nature of its aims ; thus it runs in Mr. David Laing's copy—

A N

ELEGY

IN

MEMORY

Of that Valiant Champion

Sir ROBERT GRIERSON

Of LAG.

OR,

The *Prince of Darknefs* his Lamentation for, and Commendation of his trufty and well-beloved Friend, the *Laird of Lag*, who died, Dec. 23d, 1733.

Wherein the Prince of Darknefs fets forth the Commendation of many of his best Friends, who were chief promoters of his interest and upholders of his Kingdom in the time of Perfecution.

Very ufeful and neceffary to be read by all who desire to be well informed concerning the chief Managers and management of the late Perfecuting period.

THE TENTH EDITION.

GLASGOW:

Printed by John Bryce, and Sold at his Shop, Salt-Market. 1773.

Purporting to be an expression of sorrow by
the Enemy for the loss of the services of his most
successful emissaries, chief among them Sir Robert
Grierson, the strong figure chosen by the author
is not without precedent in the history of Scottish
satirical verse.

For example, in one of the smartest of the
political squibs of Drummond of Hawthornden—
namely, that on the great English Parliamentary
leader Pym, in 1643—the sting of the piece lies in
a similar fancy. And at dates later than the
Revolution of 1688, when the quarrel had merged
into the Jacobite struggle, this form of satire was
not uncommon; and we find Bishop Burnet, the
Marquis of Wharton, and later still the Duke of
Cumberland, all dealt with in this cruel fashion;
insult sometimes being added, as in the last
instance, by the lines being set to the most lively
of reel tunes! It is interesting to note how this
grim form of joke in this particular instance
came from the *dour* Presbyterian Whigs; thus
realising, in some measure, what Jean Paul has
said, that it is only when men firmly believe in
their religion that they can ridicule it. It was
when the Evil One was most feared that he was
most caricatured. Readers of old Scots literature

are aware with what contempt the personage in question is frequently referred to—in no instance more so than in the writings of Wodrow, the historian of the Church's sufferings.[1]

A learned translator of *Faust* remarks that it has been objected to the character of Mephistopheles that he is too witty and jocular. Though not claiming to be a connoisseur of demons, the same distinguished poet gives his opinion that on this point Goethe's delineation of the character is superior to Milton's : ' It is so much more easy,' he says, ' to be sublime than to be characteristic.'

I would commend to the attention of those who agree with the accomplished scholar alluded to this Nithsdale Mephistopheles and his ' characteristic' sentiments as they are expressed in the little piece under notice, dating probably from a period some time before Goethe was born.

If this be a merit, then the anonymous Scots poet who composed the piece is entitled to his meed of appreciation.

Whoever the author may have been he had no monopoly in powerful verse and grotesque imagery.

[1] ' On the whole,' writes the Rev. Robert Wodrow, ' the devil is a great fool, and outshoots himself oft when he thinks he has poor believers on the haunch.'—*Analecta.*

Scots writers in the old time are known, when they put their hearts into it, to have been capable of a vigour of expression and graphic touch that are of the highest rank in descriptive art.

There is nothing in the *Elegy*, or perhaps anywhere else in Scots literature, more telling and malignant than the lines describing General Dalyell as—

> 'Wringing the bluid frae aff his hands,
> And scourin' them in brumstane.'

But a 'pasquil' or a satire is useless unless it be read widely; and, if possible, by the person against whom it is aimed. It was at one time believed that the *Elegy* was produced during Sir Robert Grierson's lifetime, but this appears to be very unlikely.[1]

There is nothing in the poem itself to show the authorship of this piece. It has been considered most likely to have been the work of some South Country Cameronian of the bitterest sort; and it seems highly probable that the model followed in this composition was another remarkable poem, namely, 'An Elegy upon the death of that *Famous* and *Faithful Minister* and *Martyr*, Mr. *James Renwick*, composed immediately after his execu-

[1] See Nicholson's *History of Galloway*.

tion at Edinburgh, 17th February 1688, by Mr. Alexander Shields, then Preacher of the Gospel in the Fields,' and afterwards the fanatical minister of the Cameronian Regiment already mentioned.

Some of the lines of *Lag's Elegy* are so nearly identical, in word and sentiment, with others in this piece, as to render it exceedingly probable that the latter was the model. Yet Shields himself could hardly have been the author—he died, it is believed, in the year 1700—unless the poem be of much older date than is generally supposed.

A very shrewd opinion has, however, been given on this question of authorship, which will be new and interesting to most readers.

Thomas Carlyle has drawn in his own style, with a few bold and telling strokes, a sketch of the poor old ' dominie' of Hoddam parish, a contemporary of his grandfather ' Old Thomas Carlyle,' who lived between, and after, the Rebellions.

From time to time old John Orr, the schoolmaster, used to lodge with the Carlyles; a man ' religious and enthusiastic, though in practice irregular with drink.'[1]   Thomas Carlyle heard much

---

[1] *Reminiscences by Thomas Carlyle*, ed. by J. A. Froude, 1881, vol. i. p. 38.

of this old man from his father; and he says 'a tradition of him as a man of boundless love and natural worth still [about 1831] faintly lives in Annandale.'   He was 'heartily devout yet subject to fits of irregularity; he would vanish for weeks into obscure tippling-houses, then re-appear ghastly and haggard in body and mind, shattered in health, torn with gnawing remorse.'[1]

How this poor creature brought himself, verily, almost to the brink of the grave, by carrying on his back his father's tombstone to place it on the proper spot—the pious back of Æneas had no such trying burden; how he was employed, from his especial gifts, to exorcise a spirit which had taken possession of a house; and how he actually *laid* the ghost, closeted with it, 'speaking and praying,' Carlyle has related in his quaintest manner.

And such is the portrait he draws of the man he used to affirm he had 'authentically ascertained' was the writer of *Lag's Elegy*.   This fact was communicated by Carlyle to his nephew, Mr. John Carlyle Aitken, who tells me he 'made a note of it at the time, as new and unknown to most.'

[1] *Reminiscences by Thomas Carlyle*, ed. by J. A. Froude, vol. i. p. 40.

'Old Thomas Carlyle in Brownknowe' was born in 1722 and died in 1806. His son (Carlyle's father), James Carlyle in Mainhill and Scotsbrig, was born in 1758, and must have known John Orr well.

It is not difficult to see how undesirable and unsafe it must have been that a fact of this kind should be generally known throughout the country side, and how likely it was that it should be known to the Carlyles and to very few others. Therefore, may we not say on this question of authorship, '*Aut Johannes, aut Diabolus*'? There is nothing in the dates to forbid the theory.

What Thomas Carlyle saw in this scrap of Border verse was probably no more than what is now claimed for it, namely that it is a very rough and powerful picture of popular feeling current among the class to which the writer belonged, and strong in local associations.

Carlyle's own thoughts regarding the Covenanters were, I understand, never very fully known, and, beyond an admiration for the heroic devotion and deadly earnestness which commended themselves to his nature, never expressed without reserve.

Short of absolute historical proof, probably

Thomas Carlyle's well-known tenacity of memory for everything connected with his own much-loved district of Annandale will be accepted as the strongest evidence that could be offered in this case. The subject had a peculiar interest for the Old Man of Chelsea, and—so I am informed—when he narrated these particulars he was careful to repeat them a second time, and with an emphasis, in the hope, no doubt, that they might be remembered.

Probably in every age there has existed what we have constantly presented to us in this, in varying form—namely, the anxiety of authors that some measure of the breath of Fame should pass upon them, or on their works,

'So to make them free
From dying flesh and dull mortality.'

Therefore it is a satisfaction to place on record here the claim to authorship of a famous piece of personal satire of poor John Orr ; and also, in some degree, to carry out the wish of Thomas Carlyle.[1]

[1] Another theory was at one time current, namely, that the piece was the composition of a gentleman in Dumfriesshire, who wrote it in 1770. On inquiry, however, it does not appear that any such MS. as that spoken of in floating tradition was ever in existence. Moreover, a piece written in 1770 could hardly have reached a *tenth edition* by 1773.

A recent writer says, 'In the days of Dr. John-
son, five-sixths of the reading classes were to be
found within the sound of Bow Bells. *Tom
Jones, Rasselas,* and *Pamela* were probably never
heard of beyond the four seas, till after Waterloo ;
and when all London was talking of these books,
you might probably have made a tour of England
and Scotland without meeting with a thousand
quiet people in the country who had ever heard of
either of them.'

If this be a correct picture of the country
generally with regard to literature—what must
have been the state of the rural districts of
Scotland—Nithsdale for example—towards the
end of the last century, or the beginning of the
present? It was not a state of literary destitution,
however, for there was a source of supply, much
esteemed then, and down nearly to our own day,
of a literature admirably contrived to suit the tastes
of the class of readers for whom it was intended.
The class of publications technically known as
Chap-books, and commonly called 'Penny Histories' is referred to. The *Chapmen,* or wandering
pedlars, who circulated and sold these little books,
were an institution of the period in question, and
long before it, rendered necessary by the state

of the country, bad roads, the low state of trade, and general difficulty of communication with the centres of commerce.

The chapman's pack contained all the small wares usually in demand in farm-houses and small villages, from 'miniken pins' upwards. He himself, generally a ' character,' held a position entirely his own. He saw in his constant travels much of life among the rural classes of the districts he traversed, and an important part of his stock-in-trade was the news and gossip he was able to pick up in his wanderings, to be retailed on suitable occasions to an eagerly expectant audience.

Like the minstrel of mediæval times, the Pack-man [1] was the means of circulating quantities of

[1] Some four or five years ago, there passed away, on his last journey, at the mature age of ninety-six, a noted character at Dumfries, probably the last relic of the ancient race of wandering chapmen, the errand boy of Burns. No one who conversed with him could fail to be struck with his hawk-like eye, and handsome gipsy countenance; nor to imagine, how, when at his prime, and when he carried his pack, the periodical visits of such a man, with his pithy sayings and smart repartee, must have been hailed as blessings by the dwellers in many a sleepy neighbourhood—from the lotus-eating laird, weary with glowering from his own doorstep, to the bare-footed handmaidens hungry for news from distant farm-touns.

'I knew *John Brodie*; he was shrewd and prudent,
Wisdom and cunning had their shares of him.'

verse,—or it might be good poetry. The sharp-
ness for which the packman was proverbial enabled
him to gauge with the utmost nicety the sort
of printed matter that would take with his customers. It is this branch of his trade that is
interesting.

To supply the demands which those men found
existed for literature, in a form suited to the
pockets and tastes of the people, chap-books were
produced in fabulous numbers. They were usually twenty-four page tracts, 12mo., printed on
coarse paper, the price one penny; and the subjects
the most multifarious, such as—Histories, ancient,
Scriptural, and recent; Almanacs, Dream-books,
Songs, Ballads, and sundry 'floating pieces of
Minstrelsy;' Tales, romantic, supernatural, and
humorous. But special favourites were the pro-
phetic utterances of Peden and Thomas of Ercil-
doune; also local pieces such as, *Wise Willie
and Witty Eppie* in Fife, *The Wife of Beith*
(Chaucer in a Scottish garb), and in Galloway and
Nithsdale *The Elegy on Sir Robert Grierson.*

Assuming Carlyle's theory of authorship to be
accepted, it is still doubtful when the *Elegy* first
appeared. All research on this point has failed.
While a few lines of the poem have been quoted

from time to time in books dealing with the
Covenanting age, I am not aware that it has ever
been given entire except in chap-book form.   There
is an idea among those interested in old Scots
writings that this is, if not the oldest, certainly
among the oldest of such local *folk literature*.
It could only have been written, it is thought,
and read with interest sufficient to insure popu-
larity, when the events and allusions were still
somewhat fresh in men's minds.

So, with these few words of preface, let the
reader conceive that the disguise and self-command
of the ' vagabond scholar ' have been dropped, and
the horse's hoof discovered.   Thus the Nithsdale
Mephistopheles speaks :—

WHAT fatal news is this I hear!
    On earth who shall my standard bear?
For *Lag*, who was my champion brave,
Is dead, and now laid in his grave !
The want of him is a great grief;
He was my manager in chief,
Who sought my kingdom to improve,
And to my laws he had great love.
Could such a furious fiend as I
Shed tears, my cheeks would never dry ;
But I would mourn both night and day,
'Cause *Lag* from earth is ta'en away.

It is no wonder I am sad,
A better friend I never had,
Thro' all the large tract of his time,
He never did my ways decline;
He was my constant trusty liege,
Who at all times did me oblige;
But now what shall I think or say?
By death at last he's ta'en away.

He was no coward to relent,
No man dare say he did repent
Of the good service done to me;
For as he lived so did he die.
He bore my image on his brow,
My service he did still avow;
He had no other deitie
But this world, the flesh, and me;
The thing that he delighted in,
Was what the pious folks call sin;
——, ——, and such vice,
Such pleasures were his paradise.
T' excess he drank beer and wine
Till he was drunken like a swine.
No Sabbath day regarded he,
But spent it in profanity.

But that which raised his fame so hie,
Was the good service done to me,
In bearing of a deadly fead
'Gainst people who did pray and read.
Any who reads the Scriptures thro'
I'm sure they'll find but very few
Of my best friends that's mention'd there
That can with *Grier* of *Lag* compare.

Although Cain was a bloody man,
He to *Lag's* latchets never came,
In shedding of the blood of those
Who did my laws and ways oppose.

. . . . .

Doeg, the Edomite, did slay
Four score and five priests in one day ;
But if you 'll take the will for deed,
Brave *Lag* did Doeg far exceed :
He of the royal blood was come,
Of Ahab he was a true son ;
For he did sell himself to me
To work sin and iniquitie.
Herod for me had a great zeal,
Tho' his main purpose far did fail ;
He many slew by a decree,
But did not toil so much for me
As *Lag*, who in his person went
To every place where he was sent
To persecute both man and wife,
Who he knew led a pious life.'

The plan of the *Elegy* is to devote a few lines
to each of the great actors, and to many of the
subordinates in the persecution. Nearly all those
named in the preceding pages of this sketch (and
many more) have due notice made of their exploits.
Following the opening lines on Lag, comes a long
passage on Claverhouse—

‘ Brave *Clavers* flourished in his day,
And many lives he took away ;

He to Rome's cause most firmly stood,
And drunken was with the saints' blood.

.   .   .   .   .

He riffl'd houses and did plunder
In moor and dale many a hunder :
He all the shires in south and west
With blood and rapine sore opprest.'

After mention of the shameful defeat of
Claverhouse 'near Loudon Hill,' and assistance
afforded to him against the victors, the passage
continues—

' He sought their utter overthrow
In every place where he did go.
When they were dead, such was his rage,
No less his fury could assuage
Than raise them up 'bove earth to lie
As trophies of his victory.
He was made Viscount of Dundee
For venturing his all for me.
By sudden fate at last he fell
At Killycrankie, near Dunkel ;
No longer could he serve me here ;
But *Lag* survived for many a year.' . . .

Then 'Charles Stewart' is dealt with in terms
equally incisive.   After describing, in very minute
detail, the manner of his private life and the
most prominent incidents of his reign, his alleged
treachery at Scone and Dunfermline are touched
upon.   The poet ends his description of Charles ii.

with an allusion to the story, current at one time,
and discussed by Lord Macaulay, that the king
met his death by poison at the hands of his brother,
the Duke of York.

> ‘ But kindness he did ever bear
> To all the Popish far and near.
> No Pope in Rome did ever dwell
> That could this noble prince excell.
> For in a word he did advance
> My kingdom more than Rome or France.
> He reigned long, but at the last
> His brother York gave him a cast ;
> He poisoned him, and made him die,
> And sent him home to my country,
> To Tophet, that’s both wide and large,
> Which he choos’d for his heritage.’

After passing in review Middleton, Fletcher,
Provost Mill of Linlithgow, Sir James Turner,
General Dalyell, Nisbet of Dirleton, Sir George
Mackenzie, Rothes, Monmouth, Bruce of Earls-
hall and others, we come to the Duke of York,
who of course meets with the sharpest treatment.

> ‘ For he black Popery did profess ;
> In Scotland he set up the mass.
>
> .   .   .   .
>
> For he intended in short time
> To make Pop’ry thro’ Scotland shine
> That from the greatest to the least,
> All men should serve the Romish beast.

All Protestants he did despise
And many slew without assize
By hellish soldiers, my drudges
Whom he empower'd in place of judges.'

Queensberry, Milton Maxwell, Irving of Bonshaw, Annandale, Westerhall, Winram, Laurie
of Maxwelton, and 'tree-legged Duncan Grant,'
with Archbishop Sharp and Lauderdale, are grouped
as a grim and dusky background, for the darker
figure of Lag; all of them having—

'From Sixty to the Revolution
Imbru'd their hands in persecution.
None forwarder among them all
Than noble *Grierson* of *Lag Hall*,
Whose worthy actions make him fit
In the great chair now to sit
'Bove Korah and his company.'

Then follow in detail instances of the services
which had gained for Sir Robert this pre-eminence
above all the others mentioned in the black catalogue. The Wigtown affair of course is not
forgotten. It is not necessary to give the exposi-
tion of Roman Catholic doctrine with which this
tract closes, after it has brought the Laird of Lag's
career to an end in these lines—

'He clave as closely to my law
As any man I ever saw :

In Atheism he his days did spend
Until his time drew near an end.
Then for the fashion he did say,
That he was of the Popish way;
Because a priest made him believe
That he to him would pardon give;
And would from Purgatory bring
Him to a place where he would sing.
But that was but a forged lie
For *Lag* lives hot and bien with me.'

Without stretching a similitude too far, it may perhaps be permitted to compare with this last line the famous passage in *Faust*—' Hither to me !'

The final page of this tract is occupied with a very sweet little hymn entitled *The Pearl of Great Price*,—an incongruous mixture; but the object of the poem was no doubt conceived to be the encouragement of well-doing, by showing the punishment of grievous wickedness in high places.

This remarkable poem competed not unsuccessfully for public favour with other choice specimens of local chap literature current in the South-West, notably *The Ghost of Maxwell, the Laird of Cool, and the Minister of Innerwick; Peden's Prophecies;* and *The Long Pack.* At the date mentioned in the first pages of this Sketch—that is some five-and-forty years ago—these books were

circulated in the basket of a poor old wanderer,
Katey Pickering by name, and bought and read
with the utmost avidity. Probably nothing from
the pen of Mrs. Radcliffe ever succeeded in producing such flesh-creeping terror as some of the
situations in the last-named tract, which is probably
of older date than that usually assigned to it.

Sir Walter Scott could hardly fail to be interested in such books, and he has himself said
that, at a very early age he had collected and
bound up 'several volumes' of such trifles, and
entertained the idea of writing something on the
subject some day.[1]

Therefore, when in after years he came to write
of Sir Robert Grierson and the old persecutors,
and had need of characteristic bits of description,
he had not far to seek for them. In reference to
one of the principal scenes of that rare piece of
narrative (which forms the subject of the following
chapter) in which Sir Walter has skilfully introduced many of the personages who acquired an
evil reputation in the Covenanting age, the novelist
has given the authority[2] for the lineaments conferred on certain of them. But in the case of

[1] Lockhart's *Life of Scott*, vol. i. p. 122.

[2] Notes to *Redgauntlet*.

others of the group it will perhaps be found, if the comparison be made, that the peculiarities ' condescended ' on are, in effect, those given to the same individuals in the *Elegy*.

In recent times this piece has found interested readers among those whose studies embrace the relics of a remarkable time, and the feelings and manners which the events of that period were instrumental in producing and moulding.

'REDGAUNTLET:' WANDERING WILLIE'S TALE.

Wandering Willie and his Tale!—the wildest and most rueful of dreams, told by such a person and in such a dialect! With posterity, assuredly this novel will yield in interest to none of the series.

JOHN GIBSON LOCKHART.

CHAPTER VIII.

THE story of *Redgauntlet* on its first appearance fell singularly flat. It was read in Scotland and spoken of with disappointment. In England, with rare exception, it was said by the critics to be little removed from absolute trash. Several circumtances combined to make the result of this experiment in story-telling doubtful. It was written at a period when Sir Walter Scott was singularly active in the exercise of his pen, and critics—especially the English critics—affected to complain of having to review a novel by the author of *Waverley* once a quarter; so thick the stories came.

It is interesting, in view of the change of sentiment in this matter in our own time, to notice some of the opinions of the English reviewers regarding *Redgauntlet*. The digression is not altogether irrelevant, for it is well known that much

M

of Sir Walter's story is connected with the characteristics of the Grierson family—in fact, for
Redgauntlet we may read *Grierson*. Like a pack
of carrion crows these reviewers seem to have set
—as they thought—upon the worn and exhausted
author, every one eager to pick off something for
his own advantage, and to vilify what remained.

'A frivolous production,' one writer thought
the work. 'A pippin-eating world persisted in
devouring these as golden-pippins when the graft
was worn out, and long after they had degenerated
into absolute crabs.'[1]

'A story absurd in itself, and rendered more
heavy by the clumsy way in which it is told.'

Another critic meaning to be less severe, had
pleasure in stating that the novel was *not* a failure,
but before the hindmost and behind the first ;' and
was not very sanguine that it would 'add to the
author's stock in the three per cents.'[2]

A third saw in it 'the old litany of characters,
a mysterieux, an urchin, a vagrant, a rollicking
ne'er-do-well, a human blood-hound, and a tedious
old fool.'[3]

---

[1] *Westminster Review*, vol. ii. July 24th, 1824, pp. 180, 194.
[2] *New Monthly Magazine*, vol. xi. 1824, p. 95.
[3] *London Magazine*, vol. x. p. 71.

It is long since the forecast of John Gibson Lockhart regarding the future estimate of *Redgauntlet* has been fulfilled. Had there been no *Waverley* with which to make comparison, the daring experiment of introducing into a novel the 'faded Ascanius,' combined with the profound pathos of poor Peter Peebles, and the sad merriment of the life-wrecked Nanty Ewart, would have been pronounced a masterpiece.

For those who know anything of the Western Marches, the story has a relish which the keen salt air of the Solway and the pungent peat-reek of the Lochar Moss have imparted—so strongly redolent is it of both.

There is one scene which for effect will perhaps compare with anything Sir Walter Scott has written, namely that of the meeting when the reluctant Jacobite gentlemen will not be moved by any argument of the impetuous Hugh Redgauntlet to make another effort for their king.

The incident is of interest, seeing that the Laird of Lag of that day was in all probability in some way connected (as will be shown) with the last appearance of Prince Charles Edward in Scotland.

But even the most severe of the London critics

saw a gem in this novel; namely, 'Wandering Willie's Tale,' declared to be the 'best thing in the book.'

During the last few years, within which there has been among readers a noteworthy revival of interest in all Scott's prose writings, attention has been in an especial degree given to the little story incidentally introduced in the course of the narrative, and put into the mouth of the blind musician.

Praise in unstinted measure has been bestowed on this little tale by critics whose words are of the greatest weight. There is a singular consensus of opinion that this is perhaps the finest bit of prose that has come from Sir Walter's pen. It is amusing to note that the reasons assigned for thinking so, and the beauties that are detected, are as diverse as the critics themselves. One sees in it traces of Dante; another, indications of Shakespeare; others recognise in it the semblance of a wild German legend of the most enthralling sort.

Whatever the secret may be, it is certain this little story exerts a strange fascination over readers of the most severe and discriminating taste.

Thus, for example, to Mr. Leslie Stephen's judgment, as he has 'always thought and frequently said,' it is ' the most consummate bit of work of its kind with which he is acquainted, and gives the best impression of Scott's skill as a story-teller : ' he adds, ' I almost know it by heart.'

Mr. Ruskin is one of the most ardent admirers of ' Willie's Tale ; ' and *his* theory regarding the secret of its charm, which I am permitted to quote, will certainly be interesting to the reader. Thus he writes :—

' I think the reason that everybody likes " Willie's Tale " is principally that it is so short that they have time to read it, and so exciting all through that they attend completely to it.

' The great works [of Scott] require far closer attention in their intricate design and beautifully quiet execution ; and now-a-days nobody has leisure to understand anything,—they like to have something to dream idly over—or rush through.

' In the second place, it is all of Scott's best. Few of the novels are without scenes either impossible to rational imagination, or a little padded and insipid. Sydney Smith thus condemns the whole of the *Pirate*, and I do not myself contend for the great leap out of the cave in *Old Mortality*; the Bailie's battle, or suspension in *Rob Roy*; or the caricature of Margaret's father in *Nigel*. But every word of "Willie's Tale" is as natural as the best of Burns, with a grandeur in its main scene equal to Dante—and the waking by the grave-stones in the dew is as probable as it is sweet and skilful in composition. Nevertheless, the really fine and carefully wrought pieces of the novels them-selves go far beyond it—the end of *Redgauntlet* 'tself, for instance.'[1]

Again, on another occasion, on the subject of dialect, Mr. Ruskin writes:—'I will not believe in anything to match "Willie's Tale."'[2]

The hero of this marvellous piece of story-telling, it is hardly necessary to say, is none other than Sir Robert Grierson, the old persecutor; therefore, I think I cannot err if I give here the narrative entire, just as the blind fiddler told it to Darsie Latimer as they trudged along the road together by the shore of the Solway.

---

[1] Mr. Ruskin to the present writer, 24th Jan. 1885.
[2] *Ibid.* 10th Nov. 1881.

Wandering Willie's Tale.

Ye maun have heard of Sir Robert Redgauntlet
of that Ilk, who lived in these parts before the
dear years. The country will lang mind him;
and our fathers used to draw breath thick if ever
they heard him named. He was out wi' the
Hielandmen in Montrose's time; and again he
was in the hills wi' Glencairn in the saxteen
hundred and fifty-twa; and sae when King Charles
the Second came in, wha was in sic favour as the
Laird of Redgauntlet? He was knighted at
Lonon court, wi' the king's ain sword; and being
a red-hot prelatist, he came down here, rampaug-
ing like a lion, with commissions of lieutenancy,
and of lunacy for what I ken, to put down a' the
Whigs and Covenanters in the country. Wild
wark they made of it; for the Whigs were as
dour as the Cavaliers were fierce, and it was which
should first tire the other. Redgauntlet was aye
for the strong-hand; and his name is kenn'd as
wide in the country as Claverhouse's or Tam
Dalyell's. Glen, nor dargle, nor mountain, nor
cave, could hide the puir hill-folk when Redgauntlet was out with bugle and bloodhound after

them, as if they had been sae mony deer. And troth when they fand them, they didna mak muckle mair ceremony than a Hielandman wi' a roe-buck—It was just, 'Will ye tak the test?'— if not, 'Make ready—present—fire!'—and there lay the recusant.

Far and wide was Sir Robert hated and feared. Men thought he had a direct compact with Satan —that he was proof against steel—and that bullets happed aff his buff-coat like hailstanes from a hearth—that he had a mear that would turn a hare on the side of Carrifra-gawns ¹—and muckle to the same purpose, of whilk mair anon. The best blessing they wared on him was, 'De'il scowp wi' Redgauntlet!' He wasna a bad master to his ain folk though, and was weel aneugh liked by his tenants; and as for the lackies and troopers that raid out wi' him to the *persecutions*, as the Whigs ca'd these killing times, they wad hae drunken themsells blind to his health at ony time.

Now ye are to ken that my gudesire lived on Redgauntlet's grund—they ca' the place Primrose-Knowe. We had lived on the grund, and under the Redgauntlets, since the riding days, and lang before. It was a pleasant bit; and I think the

¹ A precipitous side of a mountain in Moffatdale.

air is callerer and fresher there than onywhere else
in the country. It's a' deserted now; and I sat
on the broken door-cheek three days since, and
was glad I couldna see the plight the place was in;
but that's a' wide o' the mark. There dwelt my
gudesire, Steenie Steenson, a rambling, rattling
chiel' he had been in his young days, and could
play weel on the pipes; he was famous at
'Hoopers and Girders'—a' Cumberland couldna touch him at 'Jockie Lattin'—and he had
the finest finger for the back-lill between Berwick
and Carlisle. The like o' Steenie wasna the sort
that they made Whigs o'. And so he became a
Tory, as they ca' it, which we now ca' Jacobites,
just out of a kind of needcessity, that he might
belang to some side or other. He had nae ill-will
to the Whig bodies, and likedna to see the blude
rin, though, being obliged to follow Sir Robert in
hunting and hosting, watching and warding, he
saw muckle mischief, and maybe did some, that
he couldna avoid.

Now Steenie was a kind of favourite with his
master, and kenn'd a' the folks about the castle,
and was often sent for to play the pipes when
they were at their merriment. Auld Dougal
MacCallum, the butler, that had followed Sir

Robert through gude and ill, thick and thin,
pool and stream, was specially fond of the pipes,
and aye gae my gudesire his gude word wi' the
Laird; for Dougal could turn his master round
his finger.

Weel, round came the Revolution, and it had
like to have broken the hearts baith of Dougal
and his master. But the change was not a'thegether sae great as they feared, and other folk
thought for. The Whigs made an unca crawing
what they wad do with their auld enemies, and in
special wi' Sir Robert Redgauntlet. But there
were ower mony great folks dipped in the same
doings, to make a spick and span new warld. So
Parliament passed it a' ower easy; and Sir Robert,
bating that he was held to hunting foxes instead
of Covenanters, remained just the man he was.
His revel was as loud, and his hall as weel
lighted, as ever it had been, though maybe he
lacked the fines of the non-conformists, that used
to come to stock larder and cellar; for it is certain
he began to be keener about the rents than his
tenants used to find him before, and they behoved
to be prompt to the rent-day, or else the Laird
wasna pleased. And he was sic an awsome body,
that naebody cared to anger him; for the oaths he

swore, and the rage that he used to get into, and the looks that he put on, made men sometimes think him a deevil incarnate.

Weel, my gudesire was nae manager—no that he was a very great misguider—but he hadna the saving gift, and he got twa terms rent in arrear. He got the first brash at Whitsunday put ower wi' fair words and piping; but when Martinmas came, there was a summons from the grund-officer to come wi' the rent on a day preceese, or else Steenie behoved to flitt. Sair wark he had to get the siller; but he was weel-freended, and at last he got the haill scraped thegether—a thousand merks—the maist of it was from a neighbour they ca'd Laurie Lapraik—a sly tod. Laurie had walth o' gear—could hunt wi' the hound and rin wi' the hare—and be Whig or Tory, saunt or sinner, as the wind stood. He was a professor in this Revolution warld, but he liked an orra sound and a tune on the pipes weel aneugh at a bye-time; and abune a', he thought he had gude security for the siller he lent my gudesire over the stocking at Primrose-Knowe.

Away trots my gudesire to Redgauntlet Castle wi' a heavy purse and a light heart, glad to be out of the Laird's danger. Weel, the first thing he

learned at the Castle was, that Sir Robert had
fretted himsell into a fit of the gout, because he
did not appear before twelve o'clock. It wasna
a'thegether for sake of the money, Dougal thought;
but because he didna like to part wi' my gudesire
aff the grund. Dougal was glad to see Steenie,
and brought him into the great oak parlour, and
there sat the Laird his leesome lane, excepting
that he had beside him a great, ill-favoured jack-
an-ape, that was a special pet of his; a cankered
beast it was, and mony an ill-natured trick it
played—ill to please it was, and easily angered—
ran about the haill castle, chattering and yowling,
and pinching, and biting folk, specially before
ill-weather, or disturbances in the State. Sir
Robert ca'd it Major Weir,[1] after the warlock
that was burned; and few folk liked either the
name or the conditions of the creature—they
thought there was something in it by ordinar—and
my gudesire was not just easy in mind when the
door shut on him, and he saw himself in the room
wi' naebody but the Laird, Dougal MacCallum,
and the Major, a thing that hadna chanced to him
before.

[1] A celebrated wizard, executed at Edinburgh for sorcery
and other crimes.

Sir Robert sat, or, I should say, lay, in a great armed chair, wi' his grand velvet gown, and his feet on a cradle ; for he had baith gout and gravel, and his face looked as gash and ghastly as Satan's. Major Weir sat opposite to him, in a red-laced coat, and the Laird's wig on his head ; and aye as Sir Robert girned wi' pain, the jack-an-ape girned too, like a sheep's-head between a pair of tangs— an ill-faur'd, fearsome couple they were. The Laird's buff-coat was hung on a pin behind him, and his broad-sword and his pistols within reach ; for he keepit up the auld fashion of having the weapons ready, and a horse saddled day and night, just as he used to do when he was able to loup on horseback, and away after ony of the hill-folk he could get speerings of. Some said it was for fear of the Whigs taking vengeance, but I judge it was just his auld custom—he wasna gien to fear ony-thing. The rental-book, wi' its black cover and brass clasps, was lying beside him ; and a book of sculduddry sangs was put betwixt the leaves, to keep it open at the place where it bore evidence against the Goodman of Primrose-Knowe, as behind the hand with his mails and duties. Sir Robert gave my gudesire a look, as if he wad have withered his heart in his bosom. Ye maun ken he had a way of bending his brows, that men saw the visible mark of a horse-shoe in his forehead, deep-dinted, as if it had been stamped there.

' Are ye come light-handed, ye son of a toom whistle?' said Sir Robert. ' Zounds! if you are——'

My gudesire, with as gude a countenance as he could put on, made a leg, and placed the bag of money on the table wi' a dash, like a man that does something clever. The Laird drew it to him hastily—' Is it all here, Steenie, man?'

' Your honour will find it right,' said my gude-sire.

' Here, Dougal,' said the Laird, ' gie Steenie a tass of brandy down-stairs, till I count the siller and write the receipt.'

But they werena weel out of the room, when Sir Robert gied a yelloch that garr'd the Castle rock. Back ran Dougal—in flew the livery-men—yell on yell gied the Laird, ilk ane mair awfu' than the ither. My gudesire knew not whether to stand or flee, but he ventured back into the parlour, where a' was gaun hirdy-girdie—naebody to say ' come in ' or ' gae out.' Terribly the Laird roared for cauld water to his feet, and wine to cool his throat; and, Hell, hell, hell, and its flames, was aye the word in his mouth. They brought him water, and when they plunged his swoln feet into the tub, he cried out it was burning; and folk say that it *did* bubble and sparkle like a seething cauldron. He flung the cup at Dougal's head, and said he had given him blood instead of burgundy; and, sure aneugh, the lass washed clottered blood aff the carpet the neist day. The jack-an-ape they ca'd Major Weir, it jibbered and cried as if it was mocking its master; my gudesire's head was like to turn—he forgot baith siller and receipt, and down-stairs he banged; but as he ran, the shrieks came faint and fainter; there was a deep-drawn shivering groan, and word gaed through the Castle, that the Laird was dead.

Weel, away came my gudesire, wi' his finger in his mouth, and his best hope was, that Dougal had seen the money-bag, and heard the Laird speak of writing the receipt. The young Laird, now Sir John, came from Edinburgh, to see things put to rights. Sir John and his father never gree'd weel—he had been bred an advocate, and afterwards sat in the last Scots Parliament and voted for the Union, having gotten, it was thought, a rug of the compensations—if his

father could have come out of his grave, he would
have brained him for it on his awn hearth-stane.
Some thought it was easier counting with the auld
rough Knight than the fair-spoken young ane—
but mair of that anon.

Dougal MacCallum, poor body, neither grat nor
graned, but gaed about the house looking like a
corpse, but directing, as was his duty, a' the order
of the grand funeral. Now, Dougal looked aye
waur and waur when night was coming, and was
aye the last to gang to his bed, whilk was in a
little round just opposite the chamber of dais,
whilk his master occupied while he was living, and
where he now lay in state as they ca'd it, well-
a-day! The night before the funeral, Dougal
could keep his awn counsel nae langer; he came
doun with his proud spirit, and fairly asked auld
Hutcheon to sit in his room with him for an hour.
When they were in the round, Dougal took ae
tass of brandy to himsell, and gave another to
Hutcheon, and wished him all health and lang life,
and said that, for himsell, he wasna lang for this
world; for that, every night since Sir Robert's
death, his silver call had sounded from the state
chamber, just as it used to do at nights in his lifetime, to call Dougal to help to turn him in his bed.

Dougal said, that being alone with the dead on that floor of the tower (for naebody cared to wake Sir Robert Redgauntlet like another corpse), he had never daured to answer the call, but that now his conscience checked him for neglecting his duty; for 'though death breaks service,' said MacCallum, 'it shall never break my service to Sir Robert; and I will answer his next whistle, so be you will stand by me, Hutcheon.'

Hutcheon had nae will to the wark, but he had stood by Dougal in battle and broil, and he wad not fail him at this pinch; so down the carles sat ower a stoup of brandy, and Hutcheon, who was something of a clerk, would have read a chapter of the Bible; but Dougal would hear naething but a blaud of Davie Lindsay, whilk was the waur preparation.

When midnight came, and the house was quiet as the grave, sure aneugh the silver whistle sounded as sharp and shrill as if Sir Robert was blowing it, and up got the twa auld serving-men, and tottered into the room where the dead man lay. Hutcheon saw aneugh at the first glance; for there were torches in the room, which showed him the foul fiend, in his ain shape, sitting on the Laird's coffin! Ower he cowped as if he had been dead.

He could not tell how lang he lay in a trance at the door, but when he gathered himself, he cried on his neighbour, and getting nae answer, raised the house, when Dougal was found lying dead within twa steps of the bed where his master's coffin was placed. As for the whistle, it was gaen anes and aye; but mony a time was it heard on the top of the house in the bartizan, and amang the auld chimnies and turrets, where the howlets have their nests.

Sir John hushed the matter up, and the funeral passed ower without mair bogle-wark.

But when a' was ower, and the Laird was beginning to settle his affairs, every tenant was called up for his arrears, and my gudesire for the full sum that stood against him in the rental-book. Weel, away he trots to the Castle, to tell his story, and there he is introduced to Sir John, sitting in his father's chair, in deep mourning, with weepers and hanging cravat, and a small walking rapier by his side, instead of the auld broad-sword that had a hundred-weight of steel about it, what with blade, chape, and basket-hilt. I have heard their communing so often tauld ower, that I almost think I was there mysell, though I couldna be born at the time.

(Here the Minstrel mimics, with a good deal
of humour, the flattering, conciliating tone, of the
tenant's address, and the hypocritical melancholy
of the Laird's reply. His grandfather, he said,
had, while he spoke, his eye fixed on the rental-
book, as if it were a mastiff-dog that he was afraid
would spring up and bite him.)

'I wuss ye joy, sir, of the head-seat, and the
white loaf, and the braid lairdship. Your father
was a kind man to friends and followers; muckle
grace to you, Sir John, to fill his shoon—his boots,
I suld say, for he seldom wore shoon, unless it
were muils ¹ when he had the gout.'

'Ay, Steenie,' quoth the Laird, sighing deeply,
and putting his napkin to his een, 'his was a
sudden call, and he will be missed in the country;
no time to set his house in order—weel prepared
God-ward, no doubt, which is the root of the
matter—but left us behind a tangled hesp to wind,
Steenie.—Hem! hem! We maun go to business,
Steenie; much to do and little time to do it in.'

Here he opened the fatal volume; I have heard
of a thing they call Doomsday-book—I am clear
it has been a rental of back-ganging tenants.

'Stephen,' said Sir John, still in the same soft,

¹ List slippers.

sleekit tone of voice—'Stephen Stevenson, or Steenson, ye are down here for a year's rent behind the hand—due at last term.'

Stephen. 'Please your honour, Sir John, I paid it to your father.'

Sir John. 'Ye took a receipt then, doubtless, Stephen; and can produce it?'

Stephen. 'Indeed I hadna time, an it like your honour; for nae sooner had I set doun the siller, and just as his honour, Sir Robert, that's gaen, drew it till him to count it, and write out the receipt, he was ta'en wi' the pains that removed him.'

'That was unlucky,' said Sir John, after a pause. 'But ye maybe paid it in the presence of somebody. I want but a *talis qualis* evidence, Stephen. I would go ower strictly to work with no poor man.'

Stephen. 'Troth, Sir John, there was naebody in the room but Dougal MacCallum the butler. But, as your honour kens, he has e'en followed his auld master.'

'Very unlucky again, Stephen,' said Sir John, without altering his voice a single note. 'The man to whom ye paid the money is dead—and the man who witnessed the payment is dead too—and the siller, which should have been to the fore, is neither seen nor heard tell of in the repositories. How am I to believe a' this?'

Stephen. ' I dinna ken, your honour; but there is a bit memorandum note of the very coins; for, God help me! I had to borrow out of twenty purses; and I am sure that ilka man there set down will take his grit oath for what purpose I borrowed the money.'

Sir John. ' I have little doubt ye *borrowed* the money, Steenie. It is the *payment* to my father that I want to have some proof of.'

Stephen. ' The siller maun be about the house, Sir John. And since your honour never got it, and his honour that was canna have taen it wi' him, maybe some of the family may have seen it.'

Sir John. ' We will examine the servants, Stephen; that is but reasonable.'

But lackey and lass, and page and groom, all denied stoutly that they had ever seen such a bag of money as my gudesire described. What was waur, he had unluckily not mentioned to any living soul of them his purpose of paying his rent. Ae quean had noticed something under his arm, but she took it for the pipes.

Sir John Redgauntlet ordered the servants out

of the room, and then said to my gudesire, 'Now, Steenie, ye see ye have fair play; and, as I have little doubt ye ken better where to find the siller than ony other body, I beg, in fair terms, and for your own sake, that you will end this fasherie; for, Stephen, ye maun pay or flitt.'

'The Lord forgi'e your opinion,' said Stephen, driven almost to his wits' end—'I am an honest man.'

'So am I, Stephen,' said his honour; 'and so are all the folks in the house, I hope. But if there be a knave amongst us, it must be he that tells the story he cannot prove.' He paused, and then added, mair sternly, 'If I understand your trick, sir, you want to take advantage of some malicious reports concerning things in this family, and particularly respecting my father's sudden death, thereby to cheat me out of the money, and perhaps take away my character, by insinuating that I have received the rent I am demanding.— Where do you suppose this money to be?—I insist upon knowing.'

My gudesire saw everything look so muckle against him, that he grew nearly desperate—however, he shifted from one foot to another, looked to every corner of the room, and made no answer.

'Speak out, sirrah,' said the Laird, assuming a look of his father's, a very particular ane, which he had when he was angry—it seemed as if the wrinkles of his frown made that self-same fearful shape of a horse's shoe in the middle of his brow; —'Speak out, sir! I *will* know your thoughts ;— do you suppose that I have this money ? '

'Far be it frae me to say so,' said Stephen.

'Do you charge any of my people with having taken it ? '

'I wad be laith to charge them that may be innocent,' said my gudesire ; 'and if there be any one that is guilty, I have nae proof.'

'Somewhere the money must be, if there is a word of truth in your story,' said Sir John ; 'I ask where you think it is—and demand a correct answer.'

'In hell, if you will have my thoughts of it,' said my gudesire, driven to extremity,—' in hell ! with your father, his jack-an-ape, and his silver whistle.'

Down the stairs he ran (for the parlour was nae place for him after such a word), and he heard the Laird swearing blood and wounds behind him, as fast as ever did Sir Robert, and roaring for the bailie and the baron-officer.

Away rode my gudesire to his chief creditor (him

they ca'd Laurie Lapraik), to try if he could make onything out of him ; but when he tauld his story, he got but the warst word in his wame—thief, beggar, and dyvour,[1] were the saftest terms ; and to the boot of these hard terms, Laurie brought up the auld story of his dipping his hand in the blood of God's saunts, just as if a tenant could have helped riding with the Laird, and that a laird like Sir Robert Redgauntlet. My gudesire was, by this time, far beyond the bounds of patience, and while he and Laurie were at de'il speed the liars, he was wanchancie aneugh to abuse Lapraik's doctrine as weel as the man, and said things that gar'd folks flesh grue that heard them;—he wasna just himsell, and he had lived wi' a wild set in his day.

At last they parted, and my gudesire was to ride hame through the wood of Pitmurkie, that is a' fou of black firs, as they say.—I ken the wood, but the firs may be black or white for what I can tell. At the entry of the wood there is a wild common, and on the edge of the common a little lonely change-house, that was keepit then by an ostler-wife, they suld hae ca'd her Tibbie Faw, and there puir Steenie cried for a mutchkin of brandy, for he had had no refreshment the hale day.

[1] Bankrupt.

Tibbie was earnest wi' him to take a bite of meat, but he couldna think o't, nor would he take his foot out of the stirrup, and took off the brandy wholely at twa draughts, and named a toast at each:—the first was, the memory of Sir Robert Redgauntlet, and might he never lie quiet in his grave till he had righted his poor bond-tenant; and the second was, a health to Man's Enemy, if he would but get him back the pock of siller, or tell him what came o't, for he saw the hale world was like to regard him as a thief and a cheat, and he took that waur than even the ruin of his house and hauld.

On he rode, little caring where. It was a dark night turned, and the trees made it yet darker, and he let the beast take its ain road through the wood; when, all of a sudden, from tired and wearied that it was before, the nag began to spring, and flee, and stend, that my gudesire could hardly keep the saddle—Upon the whilk, a horseman, suddenly riding up beside him, said—

'That's a mettle beast of yours, freend; will ye sell him?'—So saying, he touched the horse's neck with his riding-wand, and it fell into its auld heigh-ho of a stumbling trot—

'But his spunk's soon out of him, I think,' continued the stranger, 'and that is like mony a man's courage, that thinks he wad do great things till he come to the proof.'

My gudesire scarce listened to this, but spurred his horse, with 'Gude e'en to you, freend.'

But it's like the stranger was ane that doesna lightly yield his point; for, ride as Steenie liked, he was aye beside him at the self-same pace. At last my gudesire, Steenie Steenson, grew half-angry; and, to say the truth, half-feared.

'What is it that ye want with me, freend?' he said. 'If ye be a robber, I have nae money; if ye be a leal man, wanting company, I have nae heart to mirth or speaking; and if ye want to ken the road, I scarce ken it mysell.'

'If you will tell me your grief,' said the stranger, 'I am one that, though I have been sair misca'd in the world, am the only hand for helping my freends.'

So my gudesire, to ease his ain heart, mair than from any hope of help, told him the story from beginning to end.

'It's a hard pinch,' said the stranger; 'but I think I can help you.'

'If you could lend the money, sir, and take a lang day—I ken nae other help on earth,' said my gudesire.

' But there may be some under the earth,' said
the stranger. 'Come, I'll be frank wi' ye; I
could lend you the money on bond, but you would
maybe scruple my terms.   Now, I can tell you,
that your auld Laird is disturbed in his grave by
your curses, and the wailing of your family, and—
if ye daur venture to go to see him, he will give
you the receipt.'

My gudesire's hair stood on end at this proposal,
but he thought his companion might be some
humoursome chield that was trying to frighten
him, and might end with lending him the money.
Besides, he was bauld wi' brandy, and desperate
wi' distress; and he said, he had courage to go to
the gate of hell, and a step farther, for that receipt.
—The stranger laughed.

Weel, they rode on through the thickest of the
wood, when, all of a sudden, the horse stopped at
the door of a great house; and, but that he knew
the place was ten miles off, my father would have
thought he was at Redgauntlet Castle. They rode
into the outer court-yard, through the muckle
faulding yetts, and aneath the auld portcullis; and
the whole front of the house was lighted, and there
were pipes and fiddles, and as much dancing and
deray within as used to be in Sir Robert's house

at Pace and Yule, and such high seasons. They lap off, and my gudesire, as seemed to him, fastened his horse to the very ring he had tied him to that morning, when he gaed to wait on the young Sir John.

'God!' said my gudesire, 'if Sir Robert's death be but a dream!'

He knocked at the ha' door, just as he was wont, and his auld acquaintance, Dougal MacCallum, just after his wont too,—came to open the door, and said, 'Piper Steenie, are ye there, lad? Sir Robert has been crying for you.'

My gudesire was like a man in a dream—he looked for the stranger, but he was gaen for the time. At last he just tried to say, 'Ha! Dougal Driveower, are ye living? I thought ye had been dead.'

'Never fash yoursell wi' me,' said Dougal, 'but look to yoursell; and see ye tak naething frae onybody here, neither meat, drink, or siller, except just the receipt that is your ain.'

So saying, he led the way out through halls and trances that were weel kenn'd to my gudesire, and into the auld oak parlour; and there was as much singing of profane sangs, and birling of red wine, and speaking blasphemy and sculduddry, as had ever been in Redgauntlet Castle when it was at the blithest.

But, Lord take us in keeping! what a set of ghastly revellers they were that sat round that table!—My gudesire kenn'd mony that had long before gane to their place, for often had he piped to the most part in the hall of Redgauntlet. There was the fierce Middleton, and the dissolute Rothes, and the crafty Lauderdale; and Dalyell, with his bald head and a beard to his girdle; and Earlshall, with Cameron's blude on his hand; and wild Bonshaw, that tied blessed Mr. Cargill's limbs till the blude sprung; and Dumbarton Douglas, the twice-turned traitor baith to country and king. There was the Bluidy Advocate MacKenyie, who, for his worldly wit and wisdom, had been to the rest as a god.

And there was Claverhouse, as beautiful as when he lived, with his long, dark, curled locks, streaming down over his laced buff-coat, and his left hand always on his right spule-blade,[1] to hide the wound that the silver bullet had made. He sat apart from them all, and looked at them with a melancholy, haughty countenance; while the rest hallooed, and sung, and laughed, that the room rang.

[1] Shoulder-bone.

But their smiles were fearfully contorted from time to time; and their laughter passed into such wild sounds, as made my gudesire's very nails grow blue, and chilled the marrow in his banes.

They that waited at the table were just the wicked serving-men and troopers, that had done their work and cruel bidding on earth. There was the Lang Lad of the Nethertown, that helped to take Argyle; and the Bishop's summoner that they called the De'il's Rattle-bag; and the wicked guardsmen, in their laced coats; and the savage Highland Amorites, that shed blood like water; and many a proud serving-man, haughty of heart and bloody of hand, cringing to the rich, and making them wickeder than they would be; grinding the poor to powder, when the rich had broken them to fragments. And mony, mony mair were coming and ganging, a' as busy in their vocation as if they had been alive.

Sir Robert Redgauntlet, in the midst of a' this fearful riot, cried, wi' a voice like thunder, on Steenie Piper, to come to the board-head where he was sitting; his legs stretched out before him, and swathed up with flannel, with his holster pistols aside him, and the great broad-sword rested against his chair, just as my gudesire had seen him the last

time upon earth—the very cushion for the jack-an-
ape was close to him, but the creature itsell was not
there—it wasna its hour, it's likely; for he heard
them say as he came forward,

'Is not the Major come yet?' And another
answered—

'The jack-an-ape will be here betimes the
morn.'

And when my gudesire came forward, Sir
Robert, or his ghaist, or the deevil in his like-
ness, said

'Weel, piper, hae ye settled wi' my son for
the year's rent?'

With much ado my father gat breath to say,
that Sir John would not settle without his honour's
receipt.

'Ye shall hae that for a tune of the pipes,
Steenie,' said the appearance of Sir Robert—'Play
us up "Weel hoddled, Luckie."'

Now this was a tune my gudesire learned frae a
warlock, that heard it when they were worshipping
Satan at their meetings; and my gudesire had
sometimes played it at the ranting suppers in
Redgauntlet Castle, but never very willingly; and
now he grew cauld at the very name of it, and said,
for excuse, he hadna his pipes wi' him.

'MacCallum, ye limb of Beelzebub,' said the fearfu' Sir Robert, 'bring Steenie the pipes that I am keeping for him!'

MacCallum brought a pair of pipes might have served the piper of Donald of the Isles. But he gave my gudesire a nudge as he offered them; and looking secretly and closely, Steenie saw that the chanter was of steel, and heated to a white heat; so he had fair warning not to trust his fingers with it. So he excused himself again, and said, he was faint and frightened, and had not wind aneugh to fill the bag.

'Then ye maun eat and drink, Steenie,' said the figure; 'for we do little else here; and it's ill speaking between a fou man and a fasting.'

Now these were the very words that the bloody Earl of Douglas said to keep the King's messenger in hand, while he cut the head off MacLellan of Bombie, at the Threave Castle;[1] and that put Steenie mair and mair on his guard. So he spoke up like a man, and said he came neither to eat, or drink, or make minstrelsy; but simply for his ain —to ken what was come o' the money he had paid, and to get a discharge for it; and he was so stout-

[1] The reader is referred for particulars to Pitscottie's *History of Scotland.*

hearted by this time, that he charged Sir Robert
for conscience' sake—(he had no power to say the
Holy Name)—and as he hoped for peace and rest,
to spread no snares for him, but just to give him
his ain.

The appearance gnashed its teeth and laughed,
but it took from a large pocket-book the receipt,
and handed it to Steenie.

'There is your receipt, ye pitiful cur; and for
the money, my dog-whelp of a son may go look
for it in the Cat's Cradle.'

My gudesire uttered mony thanks, and was
about to retire, when Sir Robert roared aloud—

'Stop though, thou sack-doudling son of a
whore! I am not done with thee. HERE we do
nothing for nothing; and you must return on this
very day twelvemonth, to pay your master the
homage that you owe me for my protection.'

My father's tongue was loosed of a suddenty,
and he said aloud—

'I refer mysell to God's pleasure, and not to
yours.'

He had no sooner uttered the word than all was
dark around him; and he sunk on the earth with
such a sudden shock, that he lost both breath and
sense.

How lang Steenie lay there, he could not tell;
but when he came to himsell, he was lying in the
auld kirkyard of Redgauntlet parochine, just at the
door of the family aisle, and the scutcheon of the
auld knight, Sir Robert, hanging over his head.
There was a deep morning fog on grass and gravestone around him, and his horse was feeding quietly
beside the minister's twa cows. Steenie would have
thought the whole was a dream, but he had the
receipt in his hand, fairly written and signed
by the auld Laird; only the last letters of his
name were a little disorderly, written like one
seized with sudden pain.

Sorely troubled in his mind, he left that dreary
place, rode through the mist to Redgauntlet Castle,
and with much ado he got speech of the Laird.

'Well, you dyvour bankrupt,' was the first
word, 'have you brought me my rent?'

'No,' answered my gudesire, 'I have not; but
I have brought your honour Sir Robert's receipt
for it.'

'How, sirrah?—Sir Robert's receipt!—You
told me he had not given you one.'

'Will your honour please to see if that bit line
is right?'

Sir John looked at every line, and at every

letter, with much attention; and at last, at the date, which my gudesire had not observed,—'*From my appointed place*,' he read, '*this twenty-fifth of November*.'—'What!—That is yesterday!—Villain, thou must have gone to hell for this!'

'I got it from your honour's father—whether he be in heaven or hell, I know not,' said Steenie.

'I will delate you for a warlock to the Privy Council!' said Sir John. 'I will send you to your master, the devil, with the help of a tar-barrel and a torch!'

'I intend to delate mysell to the Presbytery,' said Steenie, 'and tell them all I have seen last night, whilk are things fitter for them to judge of than a borrel¹ man like me.'

Sir John paused, composed himsell, and desired to hear the full history; and my gudesire told it him from point to point, as I have told it you— word for word, neither more nor less.

Sir John was silent again for a long time, and at last he said, very composedly—

'Steenie, this story of yours concerns the honour of many a noble family besides mine; and if it be a leasing-making, to keep yourself out of my danger, the least you can expect is to have a red-hot

¹ Rustic.

iron driven through your tongue, and that will be as
bad as scauding your fingers wi' a red-hot chanter.
But yet it may be true, Steenie; and if the money
cast up, I will not know what to think of it.—But
where shall we find the Cat's Cradle? There are
cats aneugh about the old house, but I think they
kitten without the ceremony of bed or cradle.'

'We were best ask Hutcheon,' said my gudesire; 'he kens a' the odd corners about as weel
as—another serving-man that is now gane, and that
I wad not like to name.'

Aweel, Hutcheon, when he was asked, told
them, that a ruinous turret, lang disused, next to
the clock-house, only accessible by a ladder, for
the opening was on the outside, and far above the
battlements, was called of old the Cat's Cradle.

'There will I go immediately,' said Sir John;
and he took (with what purpose, Heaven kens)
one of his father's pistols from the hall-table,
where they had lain since the night he died, and
hastened to the battlements.

It was a dangerous place to climb, for the ladder
was auld and frail, and wanted ane or twa rounds.
However, up got Sir John, and entered at the
turret door, where his body stopped the only little
light that was in the bit turret. Something flees

at him wi' a vengeance, maist dang him back ower—
bang gaed the knight's pistol, and Hutcheon, that
held the ladder, and my gudesire that stood beside
him, hears a loud skelloch. A minute after, Sir
John flings the body of the jack-an-ape down to
them, and cries that the siller is fund, and that
they should come up and help him.

And there was the bag of siller sure aneugh, and
mony orra things besides, that had been missing
for mony a day. And Sir John, when he had
riped the turret weel, led my gudesire into the
dining-parlour, and took him by the hand, and
spoke kindly to him, and said he was sorry he
should have doubted his word, and that he would
hereafter be a good master to him, to make
amends.

'And now, Steenie,' said Sir John, 'although
this vision of yours tends, on the whole, to my
father's credit, as an honest man, that he should,
even after his death, desire to see justice done to a
poor man like you, yet you are sensible that ill-
dispositioned men might make bad constructions
upon it, concerning his soul's health. So, I think,
we had better lay the hail dirdum on that ill-deedie
creature, Major Weir, and say naething about
your dream in the wood of Pitmurkie. You had

taken ower muckle brandy to be very certain about onything; and, Steenie, this receipt (his hand shook while he held it out)—it's but a queer kind of document, and we will do best, I think, to put it quietly in the fire.'

'Od, but for as queer as it is, it's a' the voucher I have for my rent,' said my gudesire, who was afraid, it may be, of losing the benefit of Sir Robert's discharge.

'I will bear the contents to your credit in the rental-book, and give you a discharge under my own hand,' said Sir John, 'and that on the spot. And, Steenie, if you can hold your tongue about this matter, you shall sit, from this term downward, at an easier rent.'

'Mony thanks to your honour,' said Steenie, who saw easily in what corner the wind sat; 'doubtless I will be conformable to all your honour's commands; only I would willingly speak wi' some powerful minister on the subject, for I do not like the sort of soumons of appointment whilk your honour's father——'

'Do not call the phantom my father!' said Sir John, interrupting him.

'Weel, then, the thing that was so like him,' said my gudesire; 'he spoke of my coming

back to see him this time twelvemonth, and it's a
weight on my conscience.'

' Aweel, then,' said Sir John, 'if you be so
much distressed in mind, you may speak to our
minister of the parish ; he is a douce man, regards
the honour of our family, and the mair that he
may look for some patronage from me.'

Wi' that, my father readily agreed that the
receipt should be burnt, and the Laird threw it
into the chimney with his ain hand. Burn it
would not for them, though ; but away it flew up
the lumm, wi' a lang train of sparks at its tail,
and a hissing noise like a squib.

My gudesire gaed down to the Manse, and the
minister, when he had heard the story, said it was
his real opinion, that though my gudesire had gaen
very far in tampering with dangerous matters, yet,
as he had refused the devil's arles (for such was
the offer of meat and drink), and had refused to
do homage by piping at his bidding, he hoped
that if he held a circumspect walk hereafter, Satan
could take little advantage by what was come and
gane.

And, indeed, my gudesire, of his ain accord,
lang forswore baith the pipes and the brandy—it
was not even till the year was out, and the fatal

day passed, that he would so much as take the
fiddle, or drink usquebaugh or tippenny.

Sir John made up his story about the jack-an-ape
as he liked himsell; and some believe till this day
there was no more in the matter than the filching
nature of the brute. Indeed ye'll no hinder some
to threap, that it was nane o' the Auld Enemy
that Dougal and Hutcheon saw in the Laird's
room, but only that wanchancie creature, the
Major, capering on the coffin; and that, as to the
blawing on the Laird's whistle that was heard after
he was dead, the filthy brute could do that as
weel as the Laird himsell, if no better.

But Heaven kens the truth, whilk first came out
by the minister's wife, after Sir John and her ain
gudeman were baith in the moulds. And then
my gudesire, wha was failed in his limbs, but not
in his judgment or memory—at least nothing to
speak of—was obliged to tell the real narrative to
his friends, for the credit of his gude name. He
might else have been charged for a warlock.

How Sir Walter came by the materials for this tale
there is not much doubt. There was, in fact, such
a story in substance regarding Sir Robert Grierson
current in Nithsdale; and so far back as 1814,

Joseph Train, to whose researches Scott was so much indebted for the raw material of many of his best pictures, had, as he himself says, printed the legend in a volume entitled *Strains of the Mountain Muse*. But there is evidence that the original discoverer was a certain Captain James Dennistoun, a writer of some local repute in Galloway. There is before me a note in his handwriting, in which he says he gave the particulars to Mr. Train.

The story, as told by Train, was connected with 'a man in the parish of New Abbey who had the lease of a farm from the Laird of Lag, and called on him one day to pay him some arrears of rent. Grierson took the money, but on account of some urgent business he did not write the farmer a discharge, but requested him to call the next day for the document, by which time 'the persecutor had breathed his last.'[1]

In this earlier version of the tale the farmer saw, in the hall of the castle to which he was mysteriously led, 'Pate Birnie, the famous fiddler of Kinghorn (whose Elegy was written by Allan Ramsay), tuning his fiddle to play after supper to a large company of ladies and gentlemen,' and he found the old Laird of Lag alone, 'seated at a

[1] *Memoir of Joseph Train*, Glasgow, 1857.

table with a large bundle of papers before him, apparently busied in arranging them.' With a few slight differences, and in simple words, the story contains the ground-work of Sir Walter's narrative.[1] Thus it has been said of Lag that, though his contemporaries represent him to have acted like a demon while in life, tradition allows him to have performed one act of justice after death.

In both narratives the interest hinges on the failure of a backgoing tenant to secure from his landlord, suddenly seized with his last illness, a receipt for the rent he had with difficulty scraped together and paid somewhat in the manner described. It may therefore be interesting to the reader to know that the very last discharge of this kind that is known to have come from old Lag's hand is still extant. It is contained in the old battered pocket-book already mentioned, forwarded to me by Sir Alexander Grierson. It is curious to note that it is really in favour of a tenant behindhand with his rent. In view of the associations connected with such a paper, it is a very remarkable and a striking document to handle. It lies before me. It is dingy in hue, not over clean, but the odour

[1] See Appendix No. IV.

that hangs round it is that of ancient leather and peat smoke—nothing more villainous.

Thus the discharge runs :—

'I, Sir Robert Grierson of Lag, Baronet grant me by these presents to have received from Andrew Davidson in Woodside, full and compleat payment of the rent of his possession in Woodside for ye Crop and year of God Jaj viic and twenty-four years being twenty pounds sterling in money and victuall, and therefore discharges him of ye s^d years rent and of all preceeding years and terms rents since he possest ye same, and have allowed him all his former receipts & got ye same reteired. In witness whereof I have subscrived these presents att Drumfries, ye tenth day of October Jaj viic & twenty eight years before these witnesses George McNaught my Servant and John Dun writer in Drumfries writer hereof.

Ro GRIERSON.

John Dun witness, George McNaught witness.'

The London reviewers already mentioned were sorely put to it when they had to admit the excellence of 'Willie's Tale.' In this plight one of them had the audacity to affirm that the plot was not original, nor Scotch. 'So recently as 1811,'

it was stated, 'a bold Sicilian was pointed out in
the streets of Messina as having gone to the devil
to get a lease from his landlord, and report adds
that he burned his fingers severely in handing the
red-hot iron ink-stand to his deceased lord.'[1]

Sir Walter Scott indeed says (in notes to *Redgauntlet*), that he had heard in his youth some
such wild tale, and he thought the hero was
Sir Robert Grierson.   But this was merely Sir
Walter's manner of stating the case.   He was
well aware of the name the Laird of Lag bore in
the South Country; and was wont to cite him
when he had occasion to portray a roistering
Cavalier of the ' unhappy Restoration ' period.[2]

---

[1] *Westminster Review*, July 1824, p. 186.   This and the
faint praise of *Redgauntlet*, so aroused the Scottish ire of
' Timothy Tickler, Esq.,' that he was constrained to exclaim—
and his words found vent in *Blackwood's Magazine*—' Heaven
help the blockhead ! how much do people care about the
opinions of the poor hacks who scribble at so much a sheet.
This particular ass finds, among other things, that Nanty Ewart
is not worthy of a passing notice, and that "Wandering Willie's
Tale " is a Sicilian story.   God pity him !'—Vol. xvi. p. 226.

[2] ' Donahoe Bertram, "the wicked Laird of Ellangowan,"
drank himself daily drunk with brimming healths to the King,
the Council, and the Bishops; held orgies with the Laird of
Lag, Theophilus Oglethorpe, and Sir James Turner, and lastly
took his grey gelding and joined Clavers at Killiecrankie.'—
Guy Mannering, i. 14.

From such materials as have been described, and with a loving appreciation of his subject, Sir Walter Scott has produced a picturesque view of old Lag as seen in the eyes of tradition.

The touch of genius has been effective to soften stern and repulsive facts. And, for the rest, the lapse of time has helped in some degree to give to certain characteristics the mellow tone they have acquired, now that Lag and his doings have long since passed into the region of folk-lore.

L'ENVOI.

—— Those who remember such old men will probably agree that the progress of time, which has withdrawn all of them from the field, has removed, at the same time, a peculiar and striking feature of ancient manners. . . . Although their political principles, had they existed in the relations of fathers, might have rendered them dangerous to the existing dynasty, yet, as we now recollect them, there could not be on the earth supposed to exist persons better qualified to sustain the capacity of innocuous and respectable grandsires.

SIR WALTER SCOTT.

CHAPTER IX.

L'ENVOI.

It has been accounted one of the most effective touches in the foregoing narrative, that the author has represented the successor of Sir Robert, the sleek and fair-spoken but grasping young advocate from Edinburgh, as, on the whole, harder to deal with and more disliked than the outrageous old persecutor infuriated by gout and contradiction.

For the purposes of his tale, Sir Walter Scott has assumed that Sir Robert was succeeded by the son who it was believed best answered the description of the character required.

Gilbert Grierson, the fourth son of Lag, it is understood, was bred a lawyer. Having figured, as has been told, along with his brother in the rebellion of '15, he afterwards became factor for the estates of the Duke of Buccleuch at Dalkeith,

P

and ultimately fourth Baronet of Lag. Some after-glimpses of him are obtained, as of his elder brother Sir William—a much more interesting figure—who did succeed to his father's estates and title.

There is nothing to show what part, if any, Sir William Grierson took in the Rebellion of '45. He was by that time an old man, and had no son to put forward in the Stuart cause, as he himself and his brother had been put forward. And it may well be that, having been 'out' and done his part, and suffered heavily, on the former occasion, it was not considered necessary that he should 'appear' again. At all events the feeling that enough had been done was strong in his relative, Richard Lowthian of Staffhold Hall, a Non-juror in Cumberland, who was a connection of Anne Musgrave, Lady Grierson.

When Prince Charles Edward occupied Dumfries—that stronghold of ultra-Whig opinion—with his army, on his way to England, he was lodged in the best house in the town in the centre of the market-place, now well known as the 'Commercial Inn.'[1] It belonged to Mr. Lowthian. Though

---

[1] The house is within a few yards of the rival 'King's Arms,' where Thomas Carlyle used to put up his beast when business brought him into town.

well affected towards the Prince's cause he deemed it prudent not to appear in the capacity of his host; and yet did not wish to seem desirous of keeping out of the way.

The expedient hit upon was ingenious, and has a touch of local colour in a high degree artistic. He managed to get himself so hopelessly drunk, that it was only a matter of decency that he should be kept back from the Prince's company; while his condition might be assumed, by an easy inference, to have some connection with his concern for the Prince's *very good health*.

Mrs. Lowthian, who could not be well accused of treason, was left to do the honours of the house; which she did with much grace, assisted by the ladies of the Dalzell family of Carnwath. Notwithstanding the temporary seclusion of the host, the supper went merry as a marriage bell; until the gaiety was rudely broken in upon by the intelligence—false as it turned out—that the Duke of Cumberland had taken Carlisle, and was advancing on Dumfries.

It is not till several years had elapsed, and the Rebellion of '45 become a memory, that we again meet with Sir Robert's successor.

Mrs. Anne Musgrave, spouse to Sir William

Grierson, had long been dead, and the childless old man was living in quiet retirement at Rockhall, well cared for by his ancient housekeeper, Isobel Graham, but heavily borne down by the accumulation of many debts, to the Crown and others, which his own and his father's troubles had left as a millstone about his neck ; when two ladies of the Musgrave family, relatives of Lady Grierson, conceived the idea of making a tour across the Border to see something of Scotland and, on the way, to make inquiry after the old Jacobite Laird of Lag.

It was only a matter of supreme import—the interests of his exiled king, for example—that would induce him to use his pen, or ask some one to do it for him; and they knew not if he were alive or dead.

They made their way to Rockhall, where they arrived about mid-day, and found the old gentleman in tolerable health; and made themselves known to him, as relatives of his wife. He was pleased to see them, and welcomed them warmly to his house. After much friendly talk there occurred a pause in the conversation. At last the Laird inquired, with some little hesitation—

' Where are ye going to dine the day ? '

The ladies, with equal uncertainty, replied—
'We—e—don't know.'

Sir William, somewhat put out by this answer,
after a moment's consideration, and putting his
hand in his pocket, remarked—

'Well—here's five shillings a-piece to ye.
Ye'll be going North, I make no doubt; and
ye'll just stop at the first inn ye come to on yer
road; and ye'll dine at my expense.'

The ladies reply—

'But we would rather dine with you, Sir
William, even if you give us only bread and cheese.'

Whereupon the Laird summoned his old cook,
and ordered her forthwith to kill a hen for
each of his guests. And when in due course
dinner was served, it consisted of a roast hen,[1]
placed before each of the ladies, green kail, and
oat-meal cakes at discretion.

[1] Miss Stirling Graham of Duntrune used to tell how Lord
Dunsinnan, the judge, on one occasion had a neighbour to
dine with him, at his house in Strathmore. Broth and two
boiled fowls were set before the two gentlemen. Just as they
were sitting down another neighbour dropped in, and another
boiled fowl was placed before him. After much pleasant
discourse the visitors mounted to ride home. Pondering on
their singular dinner, it struck them to ask their servants how
they had fared. The answer was—'Ilka ane got a hen boiled
in broe.'

It sometimes happens that graphic bits of
'character' are found where one would not be
likely to look for them, namely, in the body of
dry law-papers. When these are met with they
are singularly attractive, seeing that they are likely
to be as absolutely true as an oath can make
them. Facts must be tolerably exact when the
witness who states them has been solemnly sworn,
'kneeling, with his right hand on the holy
Evangels,' purged of partial counsel, malice, and
of all participation in advantage or hope of good'
that his testimony may bring him; as was the
formula in the old Commissary courts.

This has been the case with respect to Lag's
successor.

Some three years after the death of Sir William,
it seems a story arose that a confidential servant
and clerk of his, manager of his affairs, had also
so managed the old Baronet himself, and misled
him in his weakness, as to enrich himself to the
detriment of his patron's estate. Further, it was
alleged that so completely had this man got the
upper hand of the aged Jacobite Laird, that he
treated him with the utmost disrespect, and would
even venture, when they disagreed, to 'throw peats

¹ Or on the 'Evangelist,' as it is commonly printed.

at Sir William.' A remedy for the slander was
sought at law, and in the course of the proceedings a bulky volume of close print was produced.
It purports to be a proof taken on commission at
Edinburgh in the complaint of the gentleman in
question before the Court of Session, against the
Sheriff-Substitute of Dumfries and others.

Thus we have here and there throughout these
dreary law proceedings glimpses of the old Laird,
enfeebled by age and misfortune, that would have
been invaluable in the hands of Sir Walter Scott.

How, for instance, Mr. Richard Lowthian of
Staffold, whose wife was 'a distant relation of Sir
William Grierson's Lady,' who had been some time
dead, depones that at his best Sir William—he
considered—was a man of weak understanding;
and that during the last years of his life, both
his memory and his judgment were much impaired,
and he was liable to be imposed on. For all that,
he does not think that any one—either the complainer or any one else—*did* succeed in imposing on
him. On the other hand, one of his neighbours
could see no signs of his weakness, but found him
in his old age *as greedy of money* as when he first
knew him.

Another remembered how, when there was much

complicated talk regarding the letting of his farms, and exchanging of leases, and new conditions urged upon him, the old Laird should have come into the peat-house, where a tenant was depositing peats, as bound by the terms of his tack, and said, with keen apprehension for his interests—

' Jock, I wish I may not lose my rent by a' thir coups of tacks ¹ amang you.'

Then, some time before his death, he was in use, as the gardener of Sir John Douglas of Kelhead deponed, ' to write letters to different people on Jacobite subjects '—that is, he directed what should be written, for he was no hand with the pen.

There seems to have been no secrecy with regard to these treasons; for, when asked what he meant by ' Jacobite letters,' the deponent explained that old Sir William was frequently calling to him to give him orders, and that on these occasions he heard the Laird dictating the letters; ' and being further interrogated ' on the subject said, ' that in some of them which he heard dictated by Sir William he informed the friend to whom they were addressed, that the person whom he called *Prince Charles* was in

¹ Swaps of leases.

England, and he hoped would be there in a short time.'[1]

At an earlier stage of his career, the Laird had been in correspondence with gentlemen whose loyalty to the reigning family was not above suspicion. He had always had a keen eye for business, like his father before him.[2] The following letter, found in a bundle of other papers relating to his and his brother Gilbert's affairs, is evidence on both points. There is little doubt that it was addressed to Sir William, even though the direction on the back has been torn off—a very common measure of precaution in those days :—

' Bordeaux, *Feby.* 15*th*, 1735.

' Sir,—I had the honor of your's of the 18th of August, and now having an opportunity of a Ship to the Isle of Man, the Master of which has promised to further a Letter for me to Cumlongan,

---

[1] See Appendix No. v.

[2] Lord Fountainhall has noted how, at the most active period of Sir Robert's career, when His Majesty's Customs and Excise were rouped at Exchequer, they were ' fermed ' by Sir John Young of Leny, Boyll of Kilburn, and ' Grierson of Lag, the Hy Treasurer's brother-in-law,' for £28,000 yearly. Though there was competition, ' the Treasurer would have the others (Lag and his friends) getting it.' 8th August 1684.— *Historical Notices,* vol. ii. p. 548.

I have writ you this under cover to Mr. Young,
who will further it to you. I am sorry for the
misfortune to your Cock Partridge, whereby the
other would be useless; as also that so much of
your Wine was lost, which at first was so small a
quantity.

'Had this Ship been to proceed to Annan I
should have endeavoured to make up your loss
in both these particulars; but if a Ship comes here
from Annan or Dumfries this year I shall not be
unmindful of it, as also of a Guinea Cock and
Hen if it is possible to find them. I had an
account of the poor Lady Cowhill's[1] death
the post before I received your's. . . . Her
death hath left me with one friend fewer in
your country; but it will still be a comfort to me
if some that remain continue to mind me.

'I dare say your country now at the sitting
down of the Parliament will be very fruitfull of
news, of which I shall be heartily glad to have an
Account from you. The only news of consequence
in this place is that last post brought an Account
of the death of the Princess Sobiesky, which 'tis
feared will have no good influence on the Cheva-

[1] Maxwell of Cowhill, a family now represented by Campbell of Skerrington.

lier's affairs, but nobody can know the consequence
so soon.

'I am very much obliged to you for giving
yourself the trouble of seeing my mother when
you was in Town, and take this opportunity of
returning my hearty thanks for it.   Your's,—

'Pat. Gordon.'

The wine 'lost' on the occasion spoken of was
probably as much open to question as the loyalty
of these letter-writers.   There still remain, I am
told, some very carefully-kept accounts relating
to shipping transactions in which Sir William and
old Lag had been engaged, which leave little
doubt that they were interested in the peculiar
trade then almost universally carried on, by all in
a position to do so, in the most barefaced manner.[1]

[1] The following is a passage in a Petition addressed by the
Merchant Traffickers of Dumfries to the Convention of Royal
Burghs, dated 5th July, 1709 :—' The small trade we formerly
had is wholly inhanced and monopolized by Setts, Partnerships,
and Clubs of Gentlemen, Freeholders, and others within this
country . . . Great and considerable quantities of Brandy and
Tobacco they have run and carried ashore in several bye-creeks
on the coasts, such as at Newabbey, in the Water of Sark,
Cummertrees, and others . . . and have had a Ship of considerable burden lying off and cruzing alongst the coast full of
Brandy and Tobacco ; and which offered to sink the Queen's
Boat and any other boats except those of her own correspondence that offered to come near her.'

Then there were debts, as has been said, which
bore heavily upon Sir William.   Sometimes his
wife's relative, Richard Lowthian, relieved him
of these; at other times, Mr. Robert Cutlar, a
merchant in Dumfries, who seems to have had a
sincere regard and commiseration for the old man
in his helpless condition, would befriend him.
And, as the Kelhead gardener depones, in the
course of the legal proceedings, ' Sir William used
very frequently to drink Mr. Cutlar's health,' and
express his gratitude for his relieving him from
his debts to the Crown.   But thanks seem to have
been chiefly due, in this instance, to *Mrs.* Cutlar,[1]
whose intercession, not to let the old Jacobite
gentleman be distressed, availed so far as to cause
money to be advanced.

Though keen in looking after his interests, the
old Baronet seems to have won the affection of many
of his neighbours and dependants by his kindness
and friendly feeling towards them.[2]   For example,
it is related, in the course of this inquiry, how two
of his servants on the occasion of their marriage

---

[1] Mr. Robert Cutlar of Orroland had married into the
ancient and honourable family of Fergusson of Craigdarroch,
already connected with the Griersons.

[2] See Appendix No. vi.

from his house of Rockhall 'got from Sir William a compliment of a feather bed and blankets and some fir wood;' and that 'Sir William was in use to bestow compliments of furniture upon his servants;' 'well on to a dozen of chairs' to one, and to another old servant 'a *vast* of furniture.'

But the lonely old man distrusted his brother Gilbert, who succeeded him. He appears among the witnesses for the respondents in this case. David Futt, the Kelhead gardener, tells very quaintly—

'That in summer 1756, Sir William Grierson went to his brother Mr. Gilbert Grierson at Dalkeith, but returned home before harvest of that year; that he (the deponent) helped him to dismount from his horse (being weary with travelling so far) into the kitchen, where he had a seat whereon he used frequently to sit, and that Sir William expressed himself very thankful that he had got home. And that he had heard Sir William at sundry times, after his home-coming, exclaim against his brother Mr. Gilbert, as if he intended something against him by confining him at Dalkeith.'

Gilbert[1] himself, in his evidence, refers to this

[1] Throughout these proceedings, which took place after Sir William's death, this gentleman is spoken of as *Mr.* Gilbert. As

incident, and to the hurried departure of the Laird from Dalkeith, mentioning that he, having to transact some business for the Duke at a farm between Edinburgh and Dalkeith, went there early in the day, and that when he returned in the afternoon, after dinner, he found his brother gone. It was insinuated that this was in some way attributable to the interference of Sir William's manager (the complainer) who had attended at Dalkeith with certain papers requiring the old Laird's sanction—in effect, the instruments by which Gilbert should undertake the payment of the Laird's debts and make provision for him, in consideration of receiving an assignation of the rents, etc., of Rockhall, under approval of Lord Shewalton, the judge.

It is but fair to add that the case, the records of which have furnished these details, so far as the report of it goes, seems to incline entirely in favour of the complainer's contention; and shows that the reasons for the refusal to admit him

already mentioned (page 136), Sir William was succeeded as 3d Baronet by his nephew Robert. Thus Gilbert should be described as 4th Baronet (not the 3d, as in all books of the Baronetage); and consequently Sir Alexander Grierson is the 9th (not the 8th) holder of the dignity.

into the Society of Procurators at Dumfries, the
original cause of the procedure, were by no means
established by the evidence. Jealousy of his
success in life, as shown by an added radiance to
his outer man, and other signs, seems to have
been at the bottom of it.[1] .

Sir Gilbert, the rebel of 1715 (whose wife was
a daughter of Colonel Maitland of the Coldstream
Regiment of Foot Guards) was an old man when
he succeeded to the estates, and afterwards to the
Baronetcy, and did not enjoy them long.[2]

His son Sir Robert succeeded him.[3] This
gentleman, commonly known as old ' Ro. Grierson '

[1] There is a tradition that this same person having on one
occasion, in the kitchen of Rockhall, ventured on some disrespect-
ful remarks concerning Sir William Grierson, Hutchison, the
body-servant of the Laird (the Hutcheon of *Redgauntlet*, as
already mentioned)—who held everything connected with the
family sacred, whatever others might think—seized him un-
ceremoniously up, and held him over the kitchen fire, and
would certainly have ' entrusted him to the care of gravity,'
had not the other servants come to his rescue. Long afterwards
the gentleman in question, then wealthy and held in respect,
aspired to be a patron of Robert Burns, who did not like him,
and wrote some bitterly severe lines upon him on the occasion
of a keenly contested election in that part of the country.

[2] He was served heir to his brother, 24th November 1760,
and died in February 1766.—See *Index of Service of Heirs*.

[3] *Ibidem.*

from his peculiar signature, closely resembling old Lag's (p. 62), was intimate with Sir Walter Scott. He was at one time a subaltern in the 11th Regiment of Foot; and it is understood he continued to enjoy for some seventy-six years his lieutenant's half-pay. It is generally believed that many of the characteristics of the Redgauntlets were taken from the peculiarities of this worthy old man, who lived to the age of 102, or, as some say, 105 years.

Especially it is understood the character of Hugh Redgauntlet, 'Rugged and Dangerous,' the fiery 'Laird of the Solway Lochs,' was modelled upon this Sir Robert Grierson in his more irascible moods. Usually the kindest and best-hearted of men, as many of his race have been, it was a small matter that would bring out the horse-shoe upon his forehead; and at such moments he was a terror to his household.

For example, he hated to see the door left ajar by persons leaving his room. On one occasion his bailiff was being despatched from Rockhall on some business to Dumfries, and inadvertently so offended on leaving the business room. He was entering the town when a messenger on horseback, galloping, overtook him. The Laird wanted him

back instantly. On his return he learned he *had
not shut the door*.

This fine old man, who would (as I have been
told by those who knew him) have taken any
trouble to do a kindness to those about him, out-
lived Sir Walter, and died in 1839.

His wife was Margaret, eldest daughter of
Alexander Dalzell of Glenae, by whom the Earldom of Carnwath, forfeited by his grandfather in
'15, was assumed.[1]

What is believed to be the tomb of Sir Robert
Grierson, our hero, in the old churchyard of Dunscore, is now, I am told, a mass of ruins. There
is no stone to mark his grave. There is one to
the memory of Glenriddel, his friend, and another
bearing the name of 'James Grierson,' probably
Capenoch, the faithful *cautioner*; or perhaps his
son.

The lands of Lag, in the parish of Dunscore,
have long passed away from the hands of the
Griersons.

Time's tooth, though helped by fire, has found
a tough morsel in the old Tower of Lag, built in

[1] The Earldom of Carnwath was restored to this family by
Act of Parliament in 1826.

James the Third's time, whose last inhabitant is believed to have been Sir Robert. There are still some remains which have survived the combined influences—some five-and-forty feet of the square old keep, and thirty feet in height. The striking peculiarity of this ancient tower is that there is no mark of hammer or pick upon any of the stones of which it is composed. These monstrous un-hewn blocks seem to have been built in, in silence, just as they were found; no hewing mason having been employed. It is pleasant to have to mention that these venerable ruins have received the most tender care at the hands of the proprietor of the lands. All has been done that is possible, by means of 'pointing' and iron bands, to prolong their existence.

Thomas Carlyle, jogging quietly along in his gig on his way between Craigenputtock and Dumfries, would slacken his pace, and—as a recent adventurous traveller in those parts has reminded us—his eye would rest for the moment with some feeling of solemnity on the spot where, by a tiny group of trees, a solitary tombstone marks the place where Grierson led out a brave old Covenanter to be shot.

Such feeling and the memories of earnest-minded men, which such a spot is calculated to recall, are not unwholesome at the present time, when Windbags are rife and loud of voice ; and, moreover, are effective to enhance the enjoyment of the natural beauty of scenes to which the old stories and picturesque and half-forgotten legends that go to make up this bit of mosaic have given an added interest. And the effect of this narrative of Lag and his barbarities it is hoped will be no other ; unless it be to attract some to the study of a period of Scottish history not yet fully understood.

APPENDIX.

A P P E N D I X

No. I., p. 118.

RECORDS OF THE COMMITTEE OF THE SYNOD
OF GALLOWAY, 1697.

THE following is a very brief abstract of the
Report read on the 8th June 1697 :—

' Act of the Synod of Galloway, held at Wigtown,
    April 22, 1697.
 ' The Synod considering that the former flagrant
reports and surmises are very offensive in the
bounds, and a great hindrance to the success of
the Gospel therein, and do continue and increase
against the most part of the Brethern of the
Presbyterie of Wigtown. Albeit they have been
at three severall Synods already synodically ad-
monished and rebuked therefor : and that these
things cannot be put to tryall or done away by
privy censures; they having misregarded all
former admonitions of the Synod given them,
and the plurality of the Presbyterie is accused and

not so much as a Quorum left to cognosce upon them that is accused. The affair falls in to the Synod to make Loyall inquiry into these things.'

Therefore a Committee was named, consisting of ten ministers, and three elders, gentlemen of that County, namely the lairds of Barmaghachin, Cotreoch, and Garthland, to visit in the first instance the parishes of Kirkinner, Sorbie, and Mochrum, and any others within the bounds, and to examine, exhort, rebuke, and report as they should see fit, with the full powers of the Synod.

They were to hear the ministers of each parish preach 'from his ordinarie text,' and criticise the sermon, question him, the elders, heritors, or landed gentry, and the heads of families, with regard to the relations between the minister and themselves, and his general deportment.

In the face of much opposition and violent insubordination on the part of the ministers, who hint at a 'Spanish Inquisition' and so on, the Committee carry out their instructions, as is acknowledged, with much diligence and painfulness.

The report describes a curious state of things in the four parishes inspected. Under such circumstances the sermon was not likely to be brilliant. For the most part the doctrine is 'approven in the generall, but the discourses [are] curt, lifeless, and wanting in reverence;' or 'unprepared;' or 'languid in the delivery.'

More than one of the ministers had been over *four years* settled in their parishes, but in not one instance had the Sacrament of the Lord's Supper

been administered ; in one case the minister, 'judg-
ing the people to be not as yet in case for that
solemn ordinance ;' in another, the clergyman
'desires to be deliberat' in such a matter.   In
every one of the parishes it is reported that there
are 'no utensils subservient to a communion ;'
and 'no mortifications belonging to the parish ;'
by which is meant bequests from which the
elements might be provided.

While these circumstances call forth no remark
from the inspecting Committee, they note that the
parish ministers are careful to lecture once and
preach twice each Lord's Day.   They note very
particularly the complaints against the individual
pastors—how, for instance, one was charged by his
elders that 'they heard he should have passed an
expression which they knew wanton people mis-
construed ;' and that 'he laughed at the hearing
Thomas Creighton singing psalms in secret, saying
to some people he never knew any person doing
the like but an old woman in Air.'

In the case of the minister of Mochrum, though
his elders were considered to 'want edge,' yet
they charged him with 'loose speech at table
before officers of the army ; ' and, in the matter
of a ' tithe lamb,' striking a tenant of Lord Basil
Hamilton, and 'thrusting him violently in the
breast with a cane staffe, so that he did spit blood
for two months,' until ' he was cured by *Sucutillus
Balsam*, furnished by Lady Mary Dunbar.'

Sir James Dunbar of Mochrum, among other
reasons why he could not attend the ministrations

of his parish minister, alleged, and called evidence
to show, that Sabbath-breaking was another of his
faults. A witness stated that while he himself
was lying in the fields after sermon, he 'saw Mr.
James Stewart (the minister) and his father standing among the fallen sheaves of barley, and saw
Mr. James Stewart lean one or two of the sheaves
into the stook either with his hand or foot: and
saw his father either tying or lengthening the
threads with feathers which were put upon the
stooks to frighten away fowls.' The same witness
also ' heard the minister *hiss* to his dog, whereupon
the dog pursued some sheep feeding before the
gate out of deponent's sight.'

Much more to the same purpose is recorded.

No wonder that the Laird of Bargally, an elder
of Minigaff, testified how ' the things which had
been spoken had been weighty upon his spirit.'

[A memorandum, of date 1817, attached to the MS. volume
of 51 pages 4to, from which these details are taken, bears that
it was long in the possession of the late Nath. Agnew, Esq.,
Sheriff-Clerk of the County of Wigtown, and was supposed to
have been transcribed by him from the archives of the Synod
of Galloway by his father or grandfather: and that Mr.
Agnew gave it to Mr. John Black, his Depute Sheriff-Clerk,
from whom the writer of the memorandum obtained it. In a
note by the minister of Balmaclellan, the late Rev. George
Murray, dated 23d July 1863, he states that, having looked
into the original records of the Synod of Galloway, he finds
' full reference to the Committee Report, though the document
itself seems not to be there.']

No. II., p. 136.

Acco^{TT} OF THE FFUNERALS OF MR JOHN GRIERSONE.

To JEAN SCOTT.

1730.

Feb. 23rd	2 Bottels Clarit to these as set up all night w^t ye corps	0	3	0
Do.	1 Bottel of Brandy for do. . . .	0	1	6
24th	1 Bottel of Clarit when the sear cloath was put on	0	1	6
Do.	1 Bottel Clarit when the Grave cloaths was put on	0	1	6
Do.	At the in coffining where the Ladys was, 1 Bottel Clarit, 2 Bottels white wine and 1 Bottel Cannary . .	0	6	2
Do.	In the Beg room w^t the Gentlemen before the Corps was transported 2 Bottels white wine . . .	0	3	0
Do.	When the company returned 10 Bottels Clarit	0	15	0
Do.	2 Bottels brandy for Gentlemens Serv^{ts}	0	3	0
Do.	2 Bottels Clarit to Sir Roberts . .	0	3	0
26th	1 Bottel do. to Sir Roberts . .	0	1	6
March 2d	1 Bottel do. to Sir Roberts . .	0	1	6
4th	1 Bottel do. to Sir Roberts . .	0	1	6
March 5th	In the two rooms when at meat, 22 Bottels Clarit . . .	1	13	0
Do.	ffor the Servents and Gentlemens Serv^{ts} 4 Bottels of Brandy . .	0	6	0
Do.	at night when the Gentlemen returned 25 Bottels of Clarit . .	1	17	6
Do.	2 Bottels brandy to Rockhall w^t bottels	0	3	0
6th	2 Bottels Clarit at din^r w^t Sr Walter Laurie and Cariel . . .	0	3	0
Do.	Ale from the 23d of ffeb^r till this day	1	19	6

The Intertainment.

	£	s.	d.
To 1 Baccon Ham	o	9	o
To a Rosting piece of Beef	o	6	6
To a Rost pigg	o	2	6
To 2 Rost Gease	o	3	o
To 1 Rost Turkey	o	4	o
To a Calfs head stwed w^t wine and Oysstars	o	3	6
To 2 Dish of Neats tongues	o	8	o
To 2 Dish of Capons and fowls	o	6	o
To a passtie	o	7	o
To 2 Doz^n of Tearts	o	6	o
To 2 Doz^n of Mincht pys	o	8	o
To 1 quarter of Rost Mutton	o	3	6
To Rost Veal	o	3	6
To 1 Barrel of Oysters, 6 Limmons and other pickels	o	4	o
To Eating for Tennents and Servants . . .	1	o	o

We may judge how the efforts of Jean Scott for the comfort of her guests were appreciated, by the following note, attached to these Accounts:—

'We like your wine so well that the Laird has ordered me to desire you to send with the bearer half a dozen bottles. Despatch our man quickly. Being in haste, I am your very best friend ——'

No. III., p. 148.

The following are a few of the items of expenditure on the memorable occasion referred to:—

1733.   ACCOUNT OF WINES FOR THE FUNERALS OF
SR ROBERT GRIERSONE OF LAGG.

	£	s.	d.
Decr 29th 2 Bottles Small Clarit . . .	o	3	o
Do. 2 flint glasses	o	1	4
30th 4 Bottles Small Clarit . .	o	6	o

1734.

		l	s	d
Jan^r 1st	12 Bottles Strong Clarit . . .	1	4	0
Do.	3 Bottles ffrantinak	1	6	0
Do.	3 Bottles Shirry	0	5	6
Do.	1 Bottle more Brandy . . .	0	1	6
7th	18 Double flint glasses			
Do.	1 £ double refined Shugar			
8th	4 Doz^n Strong Clarit to the Lodgeing .	4	16	0
Do.	6 Bottles ffrantinak do. . . .	0	12	0
Do.	6 Bottles Shirry do. . . .	0	11	0
Do.	6 more double flint Glasses to ye Lodgeing			
Do.	12 Bottles Strong Clarit sent out to the } Burying place . . . }	1	4	0
Do.	12 Bottles more Strong Clarit at night } to the Lodgeing . . . . }	1	4	0
9th	4 Wine glasses returned from Dunscore			
12th	2 Bottles Strong Clarit to the Lodgeing	0	4	0
Do.	10 Bottles Strong Claret w^t Carriel & } more Gentelmen . . . }	1	8	0
14	2 Bottles Clarit w^t Carriel . . .	0	4	8
	8 doz^n empty Bottles returned			
The Wines amounts to		14	5	5
The Entertainments to		6	10	0

1734. ACCOMPT OF HORSSES.

		l	s	d
Jan^r 9th	2 horsses of Lord Stormonds, 2 nights, } hay, oats, & beans . . . }	0	5	0
Do.	2 horsses 2 nights, hay, oats & beans S^r } Thomas Kirkpatrk . . . }	0	5	0
Do.	the smith for Sr Thomas horsses . .	0	2	0
	py^d to Charles Herrisse, smith, for Iron } work to the Hearse . . . }	0	5	6
	Mr. Gilberts horses	1	4	6

No. IV., p. 218.

WANDERING WILLIE.

REGARDING the character of Wandering Willie himself, the materials for the portrait appear to have been furnished by Train, principally from personal knowledge. The wanderer, it seems, was not exactly a Scotch musician. He was a Welsh-man by birth, a discharged soldier, who, with his wife and five children, traversed the north of Ireland and south-west of Scotland, wherever their music was in demand. They usually travelled on foot, accompanied by a little wicker cart, drawn by a small donkey, 'of the old gipsy kind.' The man played on the violin, his wife on the harp.

On a calm evening in the month of April 1816, Mr. Train met this company near Cree. While the blind musician gave the well-known air, ' Ken-mure's on an' awa', Willie,' he had leisure to observe his costume and general aspect, which are thus described :—

' On his legs he wore a pair of blue *rigg-an'-fur* stockings, partly drawn over the knees of his small clothes, the original part of which had been evidently worn by a person of more spacious dimensions; his vest of red plush cloth, with deep pockets hanging over the thighs . . . . The outside colour of his coat was brown, the inside yellow; it was the only part of his dress which bore any proportion at all to his person. On his head he wore the cap in old times called a *megiskie*, with a large Roman letter in front, such as was usually worn by Chattering Charlie, the last professional jester of the House of Cassilis.'

A miserable fate befell this party two nights after this chance meeting. They had been refused shelter at several farm-houses where they applied late on a Saturday night, though they offered payment for lodgings till the following Monday. Necessity compelled them to take refuge from the weather in a gravel pit near the old mill of Twynholm, but ere morning the side of the pit, which had been undermined by the removal of sand, gave way and buried them all beneath it.

Attention was called to the place the next day by the braying of the donkey.

The bodies of this unfortunate family were interred in the churchyard of Twynholm. The ass and the wicker-cart, of which the wheels were of solid wood, became the property of Tibbie Mitchell, the Borgue carrier. On the person of the soldier were found his discharge certificate, a letter from a boy at sea, some little money, and papers connected with a small property in Wales to which they were looking forward.[1]

The Harper's Hole, the scene of this tragedy,

---

[1] Here are materials for a romance; accordingly the sad tale has been made the subject of a poem entitled, *Helen, the Welsh Harper*, by the late Rev. George Murray, D.D., Minister of Balmaclellan, printed in 1868.

is still pointed out—a haunt of unearthly things in human shape.

Soon after the publication of *Redgauntlet*, Sir Walter Scott remarked to his informant, 'You will no doubt recognise an old acquaintance in the Blind Beggar. Poor fellow—I must some time or other pay a further tribute to his memory, but, you know, circumstances will not permit of my doing so at present.' Details of the wanderer's story, sent to Sir Walter in view of a second edition of *Redgauntlet*, for some cause were not made use of.[1]

No. V., p. 233.

The Last Appeal to the Prince.

The scene described towards the close of *Redgauntlet*, where the Prince refuses, with much of dignity, to take the one step his few remaining followers demand as the condition of their making a last effort, is understood in reality to have occurred in Paris, at the end of Mr. M'Namara's mission, as related in the introduction to the novel. There exists, however, a French version of the incident which has not been noticed by Mr. Ewald in his interesting *Life of Prince Charles Edward*. It is, as a dramatic situation, as telling as anything in *Redgauntlet*. A party of six Scottish gentlemen (whose names are unfortunately not given) were deputed to address the Prince, with a view to

[1] *Memoirs of Joseph Train.*

another attempt in his favour ; and waited on him, one day that M. Helvétius was with the Prince.

' Il est vrai que le Chef de ce Parti mettoit une condition à ces mêmes offres,' it is said. The Prince, however, was deaf to every argument of this sort, though the six deputies, on their knees, and with tears, implored him ' de ne pas refuser, pour une femme, une couronne qui lui étoit offerte. . . . Le Prince fut infléxible.'

' Tous les six, alors se levèrent. Celui qui avoit d'abord porté la parole, ayant tiré sa montre, lui dit: " Milord, il est telle heure. Nous vous donnons une demi-heure, pour vous décider ! . . . Voulez-vous être Roi d'Ecosse, ou, toute votre vie, jouer le rôle d'un " . . . ?

' A cela, point de réponse ; et l'orateur continua de se tenir debout, le montre à la main, vis-à-vis du Prince.

' Cinq minutes après : " Milord (reprit-il) vous n'avez plus que vingt-cinq minutes, pour vous décider ! . . . Voulez vous, encore un coup, être Roi d'Ecosse, ou toute votre vie, jouer " . . . ? etc.

' Point encore de reponse de la part du Prétendant.

' De cinq minutes en cinq minutes, même interpellation, dans la même forme et dans les mêmes termes. Et la demi-heure étant expirée sans avoir obtenu de réponse, les six députés firent une profonde réverence, se retirèrent, et ne reparurent plus.'—*Pièces Intéressantes et Peu Connues*, t. vi. p. 496.

No. VI., p. 236.

Sir William Grierson and Winifred, Countess of Nithsdale.

Everything connected with the heroic Countess of Nithsdale is of interest. The following dry details of law business, taken from the family papers, are satisfactory, in as much as they show that the heroic Lady Nithsdale was treated with some forbearance by Sir William Grierson, when he himself was far from being in a position to be generous.

' Memorial from Mr. Robert Cutlar, Merchant, Dumfries, to Mr. Gilbert Grierson at Dalkeith, dated 1758,' relates that—' William, late Earl of Nithsdale, by his Missive Letter of 29th April 1708, addressed to the said Sir Robert Grierson, desired him to procure for the Earl £100 Stg., and give it to the Countess of Nithsdale, his wife; and her Receipt should be sufficient to oblige him to repay it.'

On the 5th May 1708 Lady Nithsdale granted receipt to Sir Robert Grierson for £50 received from him ' for the Earl of Nithsdale his use.'

' 24th March 1713, Sir Robert Grierson and William his eldest son, granted Bond to W. Irving, Merchant in Dumfries, for £100 Stg., and of even date William (late) Earl of Nithsdale granted a Bond of Relief in favour of Sir Robert Grierson and his son, narrating that the money had been solely applied to his use.'

19th Dec. 1713, Sir Robert and his son paid up the bond with interest to Irving, whose claim was thus extinguished. Afterwards Sir Robert obtained 'Decreet of Adjudication against the Earl of Nithsdale (d. 1744) adjudging the Estate of Nithsdale to belong to him in payment of the equal half of the sums mentioned in the said Bond, etc., amounting to £71, 12s. 6d. Stg.'

To this decreet Sir William succeeded as his father's heir.

Thus in 1740—the narrative of 1758 continues —Sir William Grierson brought an action in the Court of Session against 'Mr. Maxwell, son and heir of the late Earl of Nithsdale, for the sum of £150 Stg.' Lord Nithsdale being still abroad in 1742, the claim was made against his son. But it is pleasant to have to record in the words of the memorial, 'no further proceedings were ever again taken for the recovery of the £50 paid to the Lady Winifred, although that course was open and clear to Sir William Grierson.'

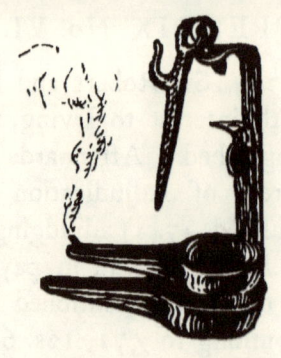

" —Donec Hodie cognominatur . .
venit nox . ."

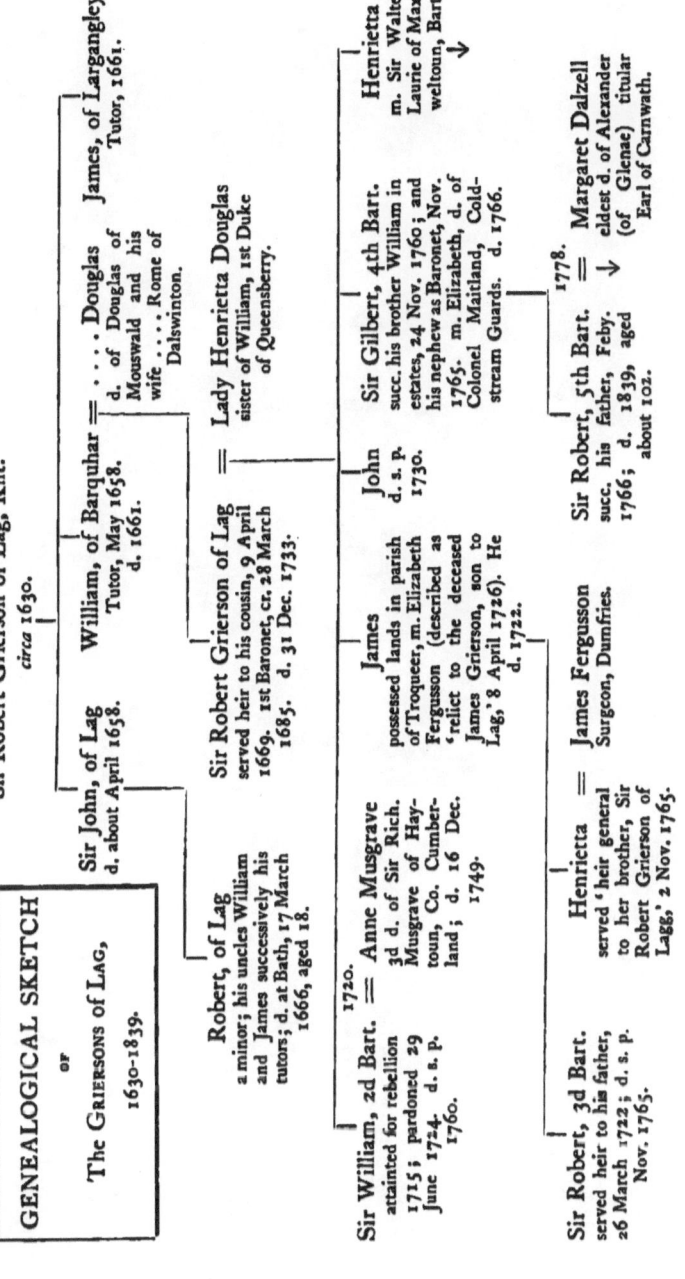

GENEALOGICAL SKETCH
OF
The GRIERSONS OF LAG,
1630–1839.

Sir Robert Grierson of Lag, Knt.
circa 1630.

Sir John, of Lag d. about April 1658.

William, of Barquhar Tutor, May 1658. d. 1661. = ... Douglas d. of Douglas of Mouswald and his wife .... Rome of Dalswinton.

James, of Largangley Tutor, 1661.

Robert, of Lag a minor; his uncles William and James successively his tutors; d. at Bath, 17 March 1666, aged 18.

Sir Robert Grierson of Lag served heir to his cousin, 9 April 1669. 1st Baronet, cr. 28 March 1685; d. 31 Dec. 1733. = Lady Henrietta Douglas sister of William, 1st Duke of Queensberry.

James possessed lands in parish of Troqueer, m. Elizabeth Fergusson (described as 'relict to the deceased James Grierson, son to Lag,' 8 April 1726). He d. 1722.

John d. s. p. 1730.

Sir Gilbert, 4th Bart. succ. his brother William in estates, 24 Nov. 1760; and his nephew as Baronet, Nov. 1765. m. Elizabeth, d. of Colonel Maitland, Coldstream Guards. d. 1766.

Henrietta m. Sir Walter Laurie of Maxweltoun, Bart. →

Sir William, 2d Bart. attainted for rebellion 1715; pardoned 29 June 1724. d. s. p. 1760. = 1720. Anne Musgrave 3d d. of Sir Rich. Musgrave of Haytoun, Co. Cumberland; d. 16 Dec. 1749.

Henrietta served 'heir general to her brother, Sir Robert Grierson of Lag,' 2 Nov. 1765. = James Fergusson Surgeon, Dumfries.

Sir Robert, 5th Bart. succ. his father, Feby. 1766; d. 1839, aged about 102. = 1778. Margaret Dalzell eldest d. of Alexander (of Glenae) titular Earl of Carnwath. →

Sir Robert, 3d Bart. served heir to his father, 26 March 1722; d. s. p. Nov. 1765.

INDEX.

INDEX

PRINTED BY T. AND A. CONSTABLE, PRINTERS TO HER MAJESTY,
AT THE EDINBURGH UNIVERSITY PRESS.